NEVER SHOW
THEM MONEY

Parker Rimes

Money often costs too much.

RALPH WALDO EMERSON

CONTENTS

CHAPTER 1

Keera Miles, assistant professor and closet psychic, suffered a lapse of concentration on her Chicago train ride home. An image of a white van appeared in her mind—and she ignored it. Big mistake. She kept gazing through the window at rooftops and wintry backyards, treating it like any normal day.

When she emerged from Sedgwick station and noticed the same van lurch forward from a parking space, she understood the earlier image. Had she held the thought longer and asked for clarification, she would have known the it was a warning—a clear signal to skip her usual station and alight at the next one. Too late now.

A second glance over her shoulder confirmed her fears. The damn thing wasn't accelerating to drive past: it stayed behind her, matching her pace.

She was a ten-minute walk from her home, a 100-year-old terrace house with solid doors, reinforced windows, and enough security to withstand an angry mob for hours. But it might as well be ten miles away. The van people didn't intend to let her get that far. That conviction was growing stronger by the second.

Keera tried to get a sense of who the occupants were and what they wanted. But her growing unease and internal agitation now blocked her perceptions. She turned around. The van stopped. The driver watched her, not moving. Behind him, the interior in tinted darkness showed nothing. At least they now knew she knew. If that counted as a plus.

They would probably move on her as soon as she turned into an empty street. Best to be unpredictable.

She quickened her steps, crossed the road, and ducked into Grinders. The cafe was empty except for two male students at one table, heads close together, fingers interlinked. Josh, the barista, was twenty years, with dark spiky hair and the soft eyes of a baby deer. He broke into a broad smile at the sight of her.

"How ya doing? The usual?"

She glanced back at the front window — no van in sight. Okay, a vivid imagination wasn't always a good thing. Hard information was better. So, Bardo, she said silently to her spirit guide, I need to know more. She held still for a second. Then another.

The answer burst upon her in a vision. The space before her split apart like a curtain unveiling a scene. A van's interior, three men and a driver. All of them Russian. All armed. None friendly. Three of them preparing to slide the side door open and jump out.

Josh placed his hands on the counter. "Are you okay?"

Outside, the van slid into view and stopped. Dirty white, no signage, no side windows, a rear-wheel cover missing. It sat at the curb, engine idling. The driver watched her through the store's glassed front, turned to somebody behind him out of sight, said something.

They were coming.

Keera withdrew her phone from her backpack, but she knew no possible help could arrive in time. She could plead with Josh to barricade the doors, front and rear; to call the cops and pray they arrived fast. He'd do it, of course he would. That would hold the Russians off for as long as it took to kick in a door and point a gun at his face. Then bruise and batter his face with knuckles and unforgiving gun barrels, just to remind him who was the real power.

There had to be an alternative.

She said, "Josh, I have to run. Can I leave my stuff with you?"

He shot out an eager hand, and she passed her pack over.

"If anyone comes in looking for me, tell them I'm in the bathroom, and I'll be out in a minute."

Josh cocked his head, but said nothing.

"I'll explain later," she added, and strode, as calmly as she could, to the rear.

A tall stack of empty milk crates sat beside the bathroom door. She dragged them further into the corridor to shield her from the view of anyone in the van. They might believe she had entered the bathroom, and wait precious minutes for her return. They might. They might also station a couple of guys at the back to box her in.

She kept moving, pushed open the rear doors to the courtyard, the metal tables unoccupied in the afternoon's chill. A gate led into a lane lined with dumpsters and spilled trash.

She clanged it open.

Two men in front of her. Leaning against a dumpster, moving their hands behind their backs so she couldn't see the beer cans.

She said, "Look, you didn't see me, right?"

Neither man responded.

"You like beer? I leave a case for you with the guy inside tomorrow if you haven't seen me."

One man brightened. "A case?"

"A whole case."

"Modelo?"

"Modelo."

He wiped a sleeve across his nose. "We saw nothing."

"Deal."

The man shuffled forward under the weight of his old army parka to shake his grimy hand with hers but Keera edged away. "I have to run. I mean it."

He lifted his hand in acknowledgment.

"Damn these boots," she muttered as she broke into a run. "Damn this coat." She stopped at the corner, looked in every direction she could. No van. She turned away from the main street and ran again. This time, faster.

"Damn that money!" she cried aloud.

When Zach's phone buzzed, he found himself talking to Sidirov.

"A friend has arrived today, and you have to meet," Sidirov said. "In person. Now."

"This isn't a good time. Some of us have to work for a living." He had no deadline that day, no compelling stories to work on, but to assent to every suggestion from this the Russian Mafia mouthpiece without question was to invite later, more violent, discourtesies.

"It doesn't work like that, Bones. We call, you make time."

Interesting. He'd given up all pretense of being an independent reporter. Now he sounded like a mob messenger. "Normally, I'd agree with you. You're important in my life."

"Ha and ha."

"I'm not joking. Right now, I'm involved in an urgent situation."

"If you don't meet us, your life will be so full of urgent situations you won't have a career."

The muscle talk was starting early. "Who do I get to meet?"

"This is not a conversation we can have over any phone. Are you at the *Post* now?"

"Sure am."

"Go outside the building and wait." Sidirov hung up.

This is how it starts. They wouldn't waltz into a room, say hi, how's it going, and leave with the money. They'd be suspicious as a cat spotting a new puppy in the house. There would be a lot of questions, most of which he couldn't answer. That would fire up more questions. They might get more forceful than he'd like. All he had was the money, but nothing beat holding a few million bucks when asking people to play nice.

A black BMW SUV drew up as Zach stepped out on the sidewalk. The blond driver emerged and came to him with an outstretched hand.

"Zach? Gennardy Sidirov."

Zach recognized his voice and gripped his hand briefly, skipping the unpleasantries.

Sidirov opened the rear door and gestured to the seat alongside another passenger, who wore close-cropped hair, a leather jacket, and the tightly wound demeanor of one who smashed heads for a living.

A third man, tall and silent, sat next to Sidirov as they drove north for a few blocks before pulling up at a diner. Inside, a lone occupant stacked chairs. Sidirov pushed the door open and handed the stacker guy money.

Minutes later, the four of them sat in a booth with god-awful coffees in front of them, while the stacker stood outside smoking, waiting, turning his back on whippy gusts. The doors locked on the inside. The backseat guy next to Zach, cozy, like a best friend, but wedging him up against the wall.

"I'm Dmitri," said the tall man who seated himself opposite Zach. He sported a military-style buzz cut across graying hair and wore a dark woolen overcoat that would have cost double the average weekly wage. Eyes dull as beach pebbles. He drew cigarettes from an inside pocket and shook the pack at Zach, who declined the offer.

"This money you mentioned to my colleague," Dmitri said after lighting up. "How much is it?"

Good question. His first idea had been to declare the whole three million, and hand it over. But the more he thought about it, the more he remembered how paranoid these Russians were. No matter what amount he told them, they'd believe a higher one was more likely. They'd assume that he, like them, would try to bilk a partner in any transaction. Best if he started low, then "found" more money if necessary. "How much?" he said. "I have approximately one million American dollars for you."

"And you have no need of this?"

"Not anymore. The money was useful as a bargaining tool. That moment has passed. It's ready for a good home."

"You have the kind heart of Boy Scout," Dmitri said. "But how is it yours to give away?"

"It ended up in my hands," Zach said. "I'd like to give it to you. No charge, no hidden fees, no ongoing relationship."

"I hear you take from Vronsky's bank. This is true?"

Of course, they would have questioned Yuri before this meeting. Their associate, currently enjoying pre-trial jail time in Phoenix, would have told them how Zach got the money. A secret organization was involved, he believed, and would have told them so. This wasn't the time to explain that the bank details and password were handed to Keera by a dead man. They would punish him for being flippant.

"It's not important how it arrived," he said now. "All I care about is that it leaves my possession. I'm sure you'll find a home for it."

"Everything has rightful home." Dmitri inhaled smoke, blew it out. "But how did it travel from Vronsky's hands to yours? This is fascinating to us."

Zach didn't respond. Let them think what they want. They wouldn't walk away from a million.

Dmitri nodded at the backseat guy, who slammed an elbow into Zach's nose with the force of a steel door.

"Jesus," Zach groaned, holding his face, inspecting his fingers for blood and finding plenty of it.

"How?" Dmitri said. "Please answer."

He was right. They smelled the money he hadn't declared. He took a breath and began his marketing pack of lies.

"The account number and password were given to me."

"Who gave this to you?"

"Yuri must have told you I can't reveal–"

Back-handed knuckles smashed his nose again. Zach waited

thirty seconds for the pain to subside before answering.

"What good would a name do you?" he said, reaching for paper napkins and jamming shreds up his nose. "You could never verify it. Take the money and avoid any unwelcome attention in the future."

"Yuri said you were government. I don't believe this. Governments never give anything back to anybody. Especially to people like us."

"I'm different, I'm more likable." Zach tilted his head back to staunch the blood flow.

"That's true. You steal money from Kazak bank and offer it to us. I dream of people like you."

"Then take the fucking money and let's part friends."

Dmitri laughed. "We'll take money, don't worry, and we'll remain friends for long time. Just in case you have short memory, let me remind you what we have already done for you. After you called Gennardy and told him that Vronsky had sold our associate Yuri to the police, we acted. Vronsky was eliminated; your life and that of your girlfriend saved. We didn't know about the money then; Yuri told us later. And, to our surprise, you made contact and offered it to us. This saved us the trouble finding you, and asking for proper payment."

Dmitri sipped his coffee, grimaced, and said to Sidirov, "Don't bring me here again." He crushed his cigarette in the saucer and didn't light another.

"We would have charged you for removing Vronsky," he said to Zach, "but instead, you have suggested new way forward. I am glad to have met you."

They wanted the rest of the money. Like he'd expected. But if he offered it too quickly, they'd up the ante. Stick to the story and see how it unfolded.

"There's no more," Zach said. "Only the million and change, all yours. Tell me how you want it. And when."

"There is plenty more, my friend. If you can take that much from one account in one day, imagine what you can do if you put your mind to it. Millions every day."

The fucker was crazy, with no way to convince him of the fact. Zach tried a new approach. "I'm just a low-level guy. I have instructions to do one thing only, which is to give this money to you. Account closed. No more. I have no means to do what you want. It's beyond my powers."

A cell beeped in Dmitri's pocket. He pulled it out, flicked eyes left-right, left-right, smiled at the screen. "Here's another thing beyond your powers," he said. "Your girlfriend. We have your girlfriend."

Jesus, no.

"It's amazing how woman can help man concentrate on important things in life, yes?"

Dmitri rummaged in a coat pocket and pulled out a slip of paper. Tossed it on the table. "This is bitcoin wallet number. The money there, by this time tomorrow. After that, we talk about weekly contribution."

Dmitri rose, the others with him. They sidled out of the booth and sauntered to the front door. As Sidirov turned the key, Dmitri looked back at Zach.

"A million a week," he said. "Easy for you, Mr. Special Agent."

The three of them laughed as they opened the door to the shivering guy out front. He scrambled inside as they drove off.

Zach watched him approach the booth and asked, "How much they pay you to look the other way?"

The guy spread his palms. "They paid peanuts, but I had no option, man. You saw what they're like. I'm just glad they didn't ice anybody in here. You wanna use the bathroom to clean up?"

"It would start the healing process, yes. But first I have to make a call. Can you give me some privacy?"

The guy moved back to the front of the room and pulled a beer from a fridge.

Zach pulled out his cell and hit Keera's number with erratic fingers, bracing himself for a Russian voice.

CHAPTER 2

Keera stopped running when she reached North Larrabee. Keera stopped running when she reached North Larrabee. By now, they—whoever they were—must have checked inside. Once they saw she was gone, the van would sweep the block in widening circles until they picked her up again. Or, if they already knew where she lived, they'd wait there. Of course they knew. They'd been waiting for her to walk home from the subway. Maybe another team was already outside her place. What she needed was a fast ride out of the neighborhood.

She turned south, away from home. The light traffic left her too exposed on the open boulevard. If the van came around the corner, they'd spot her from two hundred yards. She stopped and slipped into a furniture store doorway, peeking left and right for the van. And for a cab.

A cab appeared first, across the road, its roof light glowing. Keera launched herself from the doorway, sprinted across the median, arm raised. The cab slowed, then stopped.

"South," she told the driver. "Details in a minute."

The cabbie hit the meter, threw a U-turn at the next gap in traffic, and drove off. She picked up her cell, then realized everything would be overheard. No shield between her and the driver, and anything she said might alarm him. She slid the phone back into her pocket.

If she couldn't go home, she couldn't move in with Zach either. If these new Russians were connected to the previous ones, then they had all they needed to find both of them. Vronsky had seen both their IDs, and it was likely that Yuri had, too. That Yuri was in jail awaiting a murder trial didn't stop him from communicating with these new guys. He wanted the three million Zach had pulled from Vronsky's account; these new Russians had to be tied to him.

But Zach had willingly offered the money to them via a Russian reporter Sidirov, and he was waiting for a response. Now the answer had arrived, and it wasn't the one he'd expected. What the hell was going on?

One thing was obvious: they needed a safe haven until this was sorted. That left one option that wasn't a hotel: her parents' home—both away in Europe for a month. Her old room still set up for whenever she stayed over. The cook and the maid on leave while the house was empty. Only the gardener came by, and he stayed outside. She and Zach would have the whole place to themselves. A safe place to figure a way out of this new threat. That damn money.

With the immediate future becoming clearer, she relaxed and focused on more minor matters. She had plenty of clothes in the house, but Zach didn't.

"Nordstrom's on West Grand," she told the cabbie, and he nodded.

In menswear, her phone chirped. Zach.

"Are you okay?" His voice was raw, shaky. "They told me they have you."

"They don't. I saw them outside the café and ran before they could cover the back entrance. Found a cab." She strained to catch his tone. "What about you?"

"I'm fine." Relief poured down the line. "Sidirov took me to the boss. Dmitri. He didn't want much—just a million a week. Forever."

"What!"

A sales clerk scurried over. "Everything all right?" he asked.

"Everything's fine." She lowered her phone. "I was just surprised at the prices."

"They're very reasonable for the quality. We insist on high standards of manufacture."

"That's good to hear. I'll continue browsing then."

"Of course," he said. "Let me know if you need help."

She watched him walk off, had to be rolling his eyes.

Zach was saying, "They figured if I took money out of an account once, I could do it anytime, anywhere. For them."

Keera sagged against a clothes rack. "How do we convince them otherwise?"

"Dunno, I don't have a plan yet. I may never have a plan. Where are you now?"

"Nordstrom's. I'm getting clothes for you."

"It's not my birthday, but thanks."

"We have to stay at my parents' place until this is over. They won't know where it is. You'll need more clothes; you can't go back to your apartment. Or my place."

She visualized him mulling this over, the thoughts clanking

around, settling into place. "They're gone for the next month, in Europe. The house is empty. I have the keys. The universe is making the decision for us."

"Where is it?"

"Lake Forest."

"Of course." Zach knew better than to bring up her family wealth anymore, but sometimes, he couldn't help himself. "Lake views?"

"No. It's secluded, which is what we want. Don't we?"

"Will we have a live-in chef?"

"Stop it." His distaste for privilege surfaced again. This wasn't the time and place to have this discussion.

"Okay," Zach said. "Let's do this until we think of something better."

She gave him the address. "I'll go straight there when I finish up here. When can you get away? And, more importantly, how will you get to Lake Forest without being seen? the *Post* must be under their surveillance."

"Beats me. But I'll give the matter my undivided attention."

"You better. We need a secure base."

Keera closed the call and tried to visualize Zach sneaking out of the *Post* building. Nothing came to her. Wasn't sure if that was good or bad.

She looked around for men's clothes and found Bardo inspecting a rack of dress shirts. Nice time to manifest, when all the action was over.

"Only the wealthy wore such colors in my time," he offered as a greeting. "Of course, my position precluded me from acquiring such peacockery, but still, a monk could dream."

"Thanks for the warning," Keera said, not bothering to ask

why he waited until the last minute to warn her. He'd have his reasons, like always, and they wouldn't be made known to her.

She selected a handful of tees from a pile and placed them on top of a display rack. "Is it a good idea to move to Lake Forest? Will it be safe?"

"Nowhere is safe for long, but you can't stay where you are."

"Will we be able to evade these new Russians?" Please say yes.

"Much depends on your actions."

Gee, thanks. She pulled two pairs of jeans from a pile, guessing Zach's size, getting that she was right. "How long will this situation last? Will Zach need more than two pairs?"

Bardo smiled. "Two's plenty; he's not a fastidious dresser, as you know."

I'm only telling you what you need to know, not everything you want to know, is what he meant. Spirit guides could be so obdurate like that. She moved to the underwear section; Bardo glided alongside.

She added underwear, socks, and, spying a rack of hoodies, added a couple of them to her purchases.

"You know Zach was skeptical again, didn't want to believe your message," she said. "Why does he do this, after all we've been through? It's so wearing."

"He's obstinate by nature, contrary by design. The less you push him, the easier it is for him to accept your beliefs."

"They're more than beliefs," she said. "He's seen the concrete results of working with the other side."

"He understands that he may need your abilities to achieve victory over dark forces. But he's more comfortable with a more orthodox approach."

The trouble was, this time, there was no orthodox approach.

Zach couldn't admit to the police that he had three million of dirty money without facing an immediate investigation likely to end badly for him. With no plausible way of explaining its existence, the authorities would assume it was the proceeds of crime. Which it was: Vronsky's crimes. Dozens of kidnappings, including hers.

"It sounds like we don't have the luxury of choice," Keera said. "We can't go to the authorities; you know that."

Bardo floated over to a rack of raincoats.

"These people are asking the impossible," she said, as she joined him.

"They often do that. They get surprisingly good results, too. It's amazing what people will do when faced with stark choices."

"That's cheering." She lifted the clothes she was taking to the cashier. "Is this all I need for now?"

"I'd add something for a rainy day," Bardo said.

CHAPTER 3

When Yuri Buteyko called from his jail in Phoenix that Zachary Bones had taken money that he couldn't keep, Dmitri Rudin surprised him: "We already know. The guy's offered it to us."

"What do you mean?"

"He knew we'd ask for a fee for eliminating Vronsky, so he's made it sound like he's generous and thoughtful."

"How much has he offered?"

"He hinted at a million at least."

"There has to be more."

"That's what we thought."

Rudin posted the million-dollar bail for Yuri and flew him back to Brooklyn. The prosecution argued against any bail for a murder suspect, but the judge overruled them. Yuri had surrendered his passport, that's all. Something he could replace at the Russian embassy in a day. Money talks freely in those circles. Judges, embassy staff: they all have financial issues that need fixing

Rudin had decided to meet with Bones in Chicago and had brought his team with him, Yuri included.

"I want to see what he's made of," Rudin said. "I can spot a liar kilometers away. He may become more useful than he thinks."

Rudin hadn't said, but Yuri had discovered from the talk among the others that Rudin's career was growing precarious in Brooklyn. His penchant for unnecessary violence had brought unwelcome interest from the cops, and several of his competitors had suggested a fresh start elsewhere would be beneficial to his future, and theirs.

Since Rudin's main activity had moved from simple extortion to data theft, his base of operations was highly mobile. His data team sat in Moscow; his men on the ground in the USA sent back a list of likely targets. Rudin could monitor his operation from anywhere he liked.

Right now, he liked Chicago.

After a couple of weeks setting up a rental in Highland Park for a base, and sending watchers to scope the movements of both Bones and his girlfriend Keera Miles, Sidirov was sent to collect Bones to meet Rudin, where the reporter would learn the facts of life the Russian way.

When Rudin returned to the house and slammed the door, Yuri figured he hadn't brought any good news. The morning had promised so much. A couple of watchers planted at the girl's home, a van posted at the nearest Metro station. So simple to sweep the girl off the street and hold her while Bones completed the tasks Rudin set him.

Sidirov to bring Bones to Rudin where he'd be forced to agree to a simple suggestion: supply a steady cash stream or you never see your girl again. An unbeatable offer.

Now Rudin stalked in alone. No girl. No Sidirov. The guard Grigor, probably stationed outside.

"What happened?" Yuri asked.

"Shit happened," Rudin said, peeling off his overcoat and throwing it on the leather couch. "Those fools, those *duraki*, couldn't even grab the girlfriend. She got away."

"And Bones?"

"He was resistant to our idea."

"Even with your powers of persuasion?"

Rudin grimaced. "Even Grigor's elbow didn't change his mind. He's no pencil pusher."

"I told you, he isn't what he seems. He's undercover for some organization."

"You think that? Just because he tracked you down, and mentioned your Moscow address? Any data guy could do that."

"He knew the name of my aunt!"

"And you thought that was proof? He stumbled on it during the search process, and he pretended to know more stuff than he handed out. Old trick—you fell for it."

Yuri knew there was no convincing Rudin when he thought he was right. Most of the time it wasn't a problem—Rudin was rarely wrong, rarely diverted from his quarry. But Yuri had experienced Bones in action and had gained a hearty respect for him. And his organization.

"How much do you think Vronsky lost?" Rudin asked.

"You keep asking. He never said any number. Our team had already arranged five kidnappings so he would have taken away half a million each time after expenses at least. He was in the business a long time before I got involved, so he wasn't broke. He went crazy when he saw it gone."

"I bet. Bones offered a million. Take it or leave it. Shit, that only covers the bail I posted for you." Rudin pulled a bottle of Russian Standard off a sideboard and filled a shot glass. Swallowed the vodka in one.

"The girl is the key," Yuri said. "Bones only ever wanted the girl's safety; money never mentioned except when he stole it to force her release."

"You might be right. I had a feeling he knew he was in more trouble than he expected when we mentioned his girlfriend. But now?" Rudin poured another vodka. "By now, he knows we tried but failed to grab her. That'll cheer him up, make us look like a bunch of peasants from the steppes. He'll be more willing to take us on. That's all I need."

"How did she get away?"

"She knew, for God's sake. She spotted my guys right away. Ran into a coffee joint and straight out the back door. They never got the chance to put anyone around the perimeter."

Sounded more like they were too slow. "I told you, she's involved in a high-level surveillance operation. People are watching her all the time."

"Watching? What for? We've been here for weeks. Nothing unusual happens. She goes to university, and then she comes home. Bones arrives later in the evening. They make a lovely couple, I'm sure. And they have my money."

My money. In Rudin's mind, every dollar he could grab was already his. Anyone who blocked his path was his enemy.

"Those who watch her would have noticed our people watching her also," Yuri said. "Like last time, they may intervene. They must have warned her today."

"But they didn't interfere, did they? We'll stay on the streets, and sooner or later she'll surface. Then we take her."

Rudin wasn't giving up anytime soon. Ever since he'd discovered that Bones had stolen Vronsky's money by mysteriously learning the password, he'd grasped that Bones could be a never-ending supply of cash. Yuri hadn't even considered this. He'd hoped he'd share in a million or more, just the once. Rudin had opened his eyes to other possibilities. Which was why he was the boss.

Rudin's deal gave Yuri twenty-five percent of the initial payment, then ten percent of any continuing payments. It sounded generous. But Rudin wasn't someone who employed transparency in his accounts. He'd expect Yuri to take his word that his share was correct.

That would have to change.

◆ ◆ ◆

Zach cleaned his face in the diner's restroom. The nose was bruised but unbroken, and with the blood removed, it didn't look too weird. Swollen and yellowing, but still a working nose.

Bastards. No manners. You offer them a million bucks, and they hit you, twice, and don't even offer a ride back to work. It could have been worse, much worse: they could have grabbed Keera like they said they had. That would be game over before it started. Now, a new game, one where the rules remained unknown.

He left the diner and hailed a cab.

"The *Chicago Post*," he said to the wary cabbie scanning his face. "I fell over," he added. "It hurts to talk."

The cabbie took the hint and grunted a non-reply. Drove them away. He settled in the back and considered the Russian's offer.

What he couldn't explain to them was that obtaining Vronsky's, or anybody's, password and account number was a one-time trick. Keera had retrieved the details from a dead man—after Yuri killed him.

Zach had emptied the account, and Keera had used the fact of the missing money to force Vronsky to free her. Vronsky was shot dead two days later, and the money had remained in Zach's possession ever since.

If he played along with this Rudin, he could supply a million a week for three weeks before the money ran out. After that, who would believe him when he said there was no more?

Somehow he had to convince them only a million was available. What a crazy situation—he held too much money, and it wasn't nearly enough.

Back in the office, Howard Hossack, the newspaper's living encyclopedia, sat at his desk next to Zach's and contemplated his monitor.

"Howard," Zach said. "I have a problem."

"Always willing to oblige, dear boy, if it's humanly possible." Howard eyed Zach's shop-soiled face without comment.

How much could he tell Howard without getting him involved, and uncomfortable about it? "I appear to have become unwittingly involved with some shady characters," he said.

"How shady?"

"Russian Mafia shady."

"Ah. Russian Organized Crime, you mean. They're not so united as to be compared to the Italian Mafia." Howard pushed away from his desk. "What do you wish to know?"

"I wish I'd never heard of them but..."

Howard waited like a priest in a confessional, calm and

expectant, only missing folded hands to complete the picture.

Zach plunged ahead with the truth. "A bunch of them want money from me." There, he'd said it.

"Your money or anybody's money?" Howard unperturbed at the revelation.

"Not mine, but it's not theirs either. I've come into it, and I'd like to hand it over to them for the sake of peace. But they want more; there is no more."

"I see your dilemma."

"This money came to me—"

Howard held up a hand. "We have no client-lawyer privilege. Best we deal in generalizations."

"Okay. How do I get these vultures off my back? What's their usual area of interest? Could I dig something up that would force them to accept my offer, and leave me alone?"

"Hmm. The ROC engages in frauds of all kinds, and credit card thefts. They contain many experienced coders in their ranks, a tribute to the Russian education system, I suppose. Does this help you?"

"No."

"They're big on extortion."

"I saw that for myself."

"Violence is their preferred method of communication."

"I noticed that as well." Zach touched his aching nose with butterfly fingers.

"There is no monolithic ROC," Howard said. "They frequently splinter into small groups; loyalty is a foreign concept to them."

"So, I'm dealing with a small group of violent criminals. That's not as comforting as it sounds."

Howard turned back to his screen. "Do you have any names?"

"Gennardy Sidirov, a freelance journalist for Russian language newspapers."

Howard typed the name into an email. "Any more?"

"I met this high-up guy. Name of Dmitri."

Howard examined the ceiling for a few seconds. "Just Dmitri?"

"Yes."

"You do realize this is one of the most popular first names in Russia?"

"I can't help that. It's all I was given."

"They local Russians?"

"No, from New York."

Howard typed some more. "New York State is the home of the ROC. Also home to a thousand Dmitris. This may cost you more than you can afford."

"You charging me now"

"Don't be silly. This is way out of my area of expertise. I know this guy who can discover anything you want. But he has to eat. Do you have a budget for this?"

Zach pictured the three million in his Cayman account and said yes.

"This Dmitri," Howard said. "Is he in Chicago right now?"

"Unfortunately, yes."

"That makes it easier. If he flew, he's on a server somewhere. If he drove, he was photographed on the way. His image exists. My friend will find him."

"Your guy has access to all this?"

"He was linked with the NSA, now in business for himself. I have to assume, given the results delivered in the past, that he's kept in touch with his government contacts."

"How come you know him?"

"School chum."

Why bother asking? Howard and his old-boy network probably ran the Illuminati by now.

"Look," Howard said. "If your Dmitri is involved in the ROC then he's under surveillance. The FBI will be watching and noting the people he meets, building up a body of evidence so that they can one day nail him, and everybody he's dealt with. If you dig up stuff we can publish, even better. Long term, you'll be free of him."

Long term wasn't good. He needed a faster solution. Also, if the FBI were already watching Dmitri, then they witnessed today's meet. His name might be noted; he might be picked up for associating with Dmitri. That wouldn't be wonderful either. Freedom of the press goes only so far with the FBI.

"Howard," he said. "You're right, but I need something more immediate." He swiveled back to his desk. The first thing was to avoid meeting with Dmitri ever again. Keep his negotiating at arm's length—especially that goon's arm.

Five minutes later, after Zach had reflected on the morning's events, and his anger had grown to a hot hard knot, he called Sidirov, who took his time answering.

"Yeah?" he said eventually. Ever the polite son his mother had hoped for.

"I didn't appreciate what happened today," Zach said. "Trying to scare me with an attempt to grab my girlfriend."

"I don't know what you're talking about." Sidirov was telling him phones weren't to be trusted.

"Your guy said he had her, but he didn't. His credibility is fucked. You understand?"

Sidirov didn't reply, didn't have to. The van guys must have assumed Keera was still in the cafe when they texted Dmitri. Their overconfidence had destroyed Dmitri's smooth command of the meet. Hopefully, Dmitri's guard was now playing elbow music on the van guys' noses.

"This was a straightforward transaction," Zach said. "Then all this bullshit starts. And what gives with smacking me? You think I'm a street urchin that needs to keep in line." Fucking humiliating, that.

"I haven't a clue what you're talking about," Sidirov said. "We'll meet tomorrow, and you can get everything off your chest. How's that?"

"I gotta say that if you guys want to play it like this, I'm going to get totally uninterested in further dealings. Got it?"

Sidirov switched off rather than listen to more, but the message was delivered. That he would withdraw his offer if they continued down the violent route. And that Dmitri and his gang were clowns. Not to be trusted. Made him feel a lot better. Until he realized that Dmitri's goons had to be watching the *Post* building.

With Keera escaping them, they'd be doubly sure not to lose track of him. Especially after Sidirov passed on the latest conversation.

"Howard," he said. "I assume there's a back way out of here."

"Your life is so interesting," he said, not taking his eyes off his screen, "that I'm glad it's not mine. Take the service elevator to the basement. See if you can hitch a ride out with a delivery truck." He stopping typing, reached into his desk drawer and pulled out a Red Sox cap. "You might want this."

"Red Sox? Red Sox? Do you know what city you live in? I'll give you a clue: it's not Boston."

"Old loyalties die hard; I grew up there. I want it back, too."

Zach jammed the cap on his head and caught the service elevator. He shared it with a guy leaning on an empty two-wheeled trolley.

"You been delivering stationery supplies?" he asked.

"Coffee pods. For those espresso machines."

"You ever drunk one of those?"

"Nope."

"Keep it that way. Listen, I need to get out of this place without being seen. Can I ride in your truck for a couple of blocks?"

"You kidding?" The guy examined him more carefully. Like bad intentions might be visible if he looked hard enough.

"I'll give you a twenty, just a ride down the street."

The guy wasn't convinced. "You one of those undercover company guys making sure I don't use my delivery van for private purposes?"

"No way. There are people outside looking to, um, you know, mess with me."

"Whatcha doing in this building?"

"I'm a journalist. On the *Post*."

"You gonna do a story about me using the company van for private reasons?"

So suspicious. Whatever happened to goodwill between all men? "I wouldn't be this obvious."

"Why you hiding from these guys?"

"It's a loan shark thing. I'm late with payments."

The guy grinned unexpectedly. "Been there myself. They

don't mess about, do they?" The elevator doors rumbled open. "This way, pal."

The loading dock contained another van delivering office supplies, and one larger truck where two guys wrestled office furniture down a ramp. Coffee Guy threw the hand trolley in the back of his van and climbed in the front, Zach joining him on the other side.

Coffee Guy started the motor and said, "If anybody's in the access lane, they'll be sitting in a ten-minute zone to the right. We'll be going past them. Slide down out of sight. If they saw me come in—and I wasn't paying attention to my surroundings, you understand—then they might remember that I drove in alone."

Zach pushed his seat back and dropped into the footwell. Wished he was smaller. The Coffee Guy didn't wait for him to get comfortable, drove out of the yard and turned right.

"There's a van," he said. "One driver, one passenger. Not doing nothin'. Standing out like shirkers on a construction site."

He didn't slow until he reached the main street. "They're not moving," he said, checking the mirror. Took a right and merged with the traffic. He stopped a few blocks down the street, accepted the twenty, and waited for Zach to climb out.

"I woulda agreed faster," he said, "hadda been a Cubs cap on your head."

CHAPTER 4

Keera stood by the front door watching Zach pay off the cabbie. As he walked up the sweeping drive, she activated the gates to close behind him. He acknowledged her with a half-embarrassed wave like he'd rather not be here. Like he had a choice.

They embraced at the door; the physical contact made more precious by the afternoon's danger. She pulled back to examine his face; his nose looked like a sculptor's work in progress, small blood specks dotting his chin.

"What did they do to you?" she asked.

"Not much, they got a little impatient with me, is all."

"Bet you were too lippy when you should have stayed polite."

"It's a weakness, I admit. But in this case, they were showing me they weren't opposed to a little physicality if necessary. I wasn't trying to annoy them, that's for sure. I just wanted the deal done."

His nose had obviously engaged in the discussion, but she didn't comment on it.

Zach looked around at the oak-paneled walls, the muted floor rugs, and the hallway that widened to accommodate a curving staircase to the upper floor. "Nice place," he said. "Must've been fun playing here as a kid."

She led him to the main living area, holding hands, past the formal dining room, a study and doors that she didn't bother explaining. "We didn't live here until my teens," she said. "By then, I couldn't wait to move out, no matter how comfortable the surroundings."

The living area was a combined dining space and kitchen, with another large room leading off this where soft couches clustered around a fireplace. He'd lived in apartments smaller than this.

Her shopping bags crowded the dining table. She drew out the items she'd bought for him. "Since you only wear tees, jeans, and the occasional jacket, I didn't try for a makeover."

He pulled a pair of jeans out for inspection. "My size, amazing. Nordstrom? What are you doing paying a couple of hundred bucks for jeans?" He fingered the tees, flipped a price tag over. "Eighty-five bucks!"

"I was in a hurry. Our weekly clothes budget was not at the forefront of my mind."

"So I see. You know I'm a plain guy with plain tastes, and you headed for a high-class store?"

"I headed for a store I knew. Shall we change the subject?" The gratitude of the guy.

Zach peered into the fridge. "Not much in here."

"The house is unoccupied for the next six months. What do you expect?"

"Beer for the cleaners and gardeners. And visitors, like me."

"That's in the next fridge. The drinks fridge."

Zach opened it. "Now, that's what I call a pleasing sight. A range of beers, some white wines. Plenty of calories here; we don't need any food at all."

"Plenty of food in the larders as long as you don't mind non-perishables. The staff eat in here, and their tastes steer to the filling and flavorful. If my parents have guests, they bring in caterers. It's too nerve-wracking for our cook otherwise."

"Such problems you have."

"Shut up, Zach. Let me show you our room."

"In a minute." Zach pulled a can of Modelo in the drinks fridge and cracked it open. "It's been a hard day," he said in reply to her questioning eyebrow. "Where are the glasses? If I can't smell the beer, I miss out on half the enjoyment."

Keera opened a cupboard and handed him a glass. "We'll stay in my room. It's always kept ready for me if I stay over on weekends."

"Wait a minute. Is it all girly, like when you were a teen, with boy band posters and shit on the walls? Teddy bears on the bed?"

"Not so's you'd notice." She smiled back, letting him know she was ignoring his grumpiness. After the Russian meet, he was entitled to be that way. For a little longer.

"I have standards, you know."

"There's a guest room next to mine. More manly, it has a leather chair. Suit you?"

"Sounds like the best choice." He rummaged in the larder, beer in hand. "Hey, corn chips, salsa, the staff of life." He placed a selection of snacks on the table, pushing aside the shopping. "Wine for you?"

"Just the one," she said, taking a seat. "We need clear heads, not crazy suggestions."

They sipped and dipped for a minute or two, then Zach said, "I knew they wouldn't settle for the first amount I said, so I started with a million."

"What if they'd accepted? What were you planning to do with the other two million?" Zach was still attached to Vronsky's money. Try as he might, he hadn't had her advantages in life, and she knew the sheer amount of it kept eating at him.

When she had pointed out that keeping it would create a massive rift between them, he found a solution—paying off Yuri's pals, who'd eliminated Vronsky from their life. A kind of thanks.

Now, a lifetime's earnings sat in an offshore account, and he couldn't even give it away. He was probably thinking: the hell with this, I might as well use it. Except he'd already attracted the rats, and they would never give up this prize.

"No chance they would have accepted the first offer," Zach said. "They're incredibly suspicious people. In any case, it doesn't matter. They want a million each week now. Sounds like Yuri convinced them we were undercover secret government agents that could do anything."

"They didn't seem too afraid of incurring the wrath of this secret agency."

"Dmitri isn't convinced. Not fully. He'll expect me to send him a million bucks in bitcoins each week. If he's got you, then he knows I'll try my best. If that can't be done, then they might take what I first offered and leave. Hopefully, with the two of us unscathed by the experience."

"If you believe that, you also believe that if you're a good boy, Santa will bring you a terrific present."

"I'm trying to be positive here." He scraped a chip around the jar of salsa, crunched on it thoughtfully. "Hell of a situation," he said. "I offered them money to leave us alone, and it's all turned batshit crazy."

"Trying to make a deal with people like them is like approaching a black hole. You draw too close, and you're trapped —never to escape. Maybe we shouldn't have mentioned the money."

"We had no choice. Yuri knew of its existence, but not the amount, which has created the problem. Maybe I can convince him I'm on the level."

"Before we do anything, I need to check out this Dmitri."

"I'm doing that already. Got some of the finest sleuths in action as we speak."

"I was thinking of observing him on the astral."

Zach grinned. "Well, that'll help."

"I was thinking more like revisiting his past. It's a thought that's been pushing forward in my mind for the last few hours."

"Get some background, you mean?"

"I don't know what I'll get. I have a strong feeling that I should go back to a few years ago. Something happened that's important to us now. Don't ask me anymore. That's all I have."

"You want me to describe Dmitri for you?"

"No, I'll find him no matter what. Anyway, if I go back a few years, he may look quite different."

Zach pulled another Modelo from the fridge, not catching her eye until he'd sat down again and taken a deep draught.

"Now that we're here," he said, "we've bought some time. I can stay away from the office, email my copy. What about you?"

"Harder for me. I have students to meet and advise."

"Call in sick."

"I could, but I'd feel so bad about letting people down."

"Keera, we don't need you snatched off the street, or a lecture hall, or a tutorial room. Got it? These guys have no manners. They won't wait until you're ready."

She thought of the van people, not even bothering to check the rear exit of the cafe. "They're pretty bad at their job. I can get a cab from here."

"Sure you can. And they have guys watching your department right now. They see you get out, they talk to the cabbie, offer him money or shove a gun barrel up his nose, either way, he tells them where he picked you up. You come home that night; they're sitting around, waiting, enjoying your father's fifty-year-old whiskey." He finished the beer. "They need you to keep me doing their bidding. No chance they lose you a second time."

He was right. She'd stay here, safe, at least until she had a working sense of what they faced. Between the two of them, they'd locate Dmitri and neutralize him. Of course they would.

Zach tossed the empty salsa jar into the garbage and rummaged through the drinks fridge again. How much alcohol did he need tonight? He emerged with a hunk of cheese.

"Cheese and wine," he said. "Reminds me of our first night together."

The first night. He hadn't come on to her as she expected; he'd waited long enough for her to cast aside her hesitation and make the first move. After that, she never doubted they had been brought together for a purpose. And he still had that trick of teasing her until she was ready to explode from sexual tension. Like now.

"Cheese and wine? Perfect match." she said, hoping they

started the kissing soon. He was better than he knew.

Zach rose and pulled her to her feet, nuzzled her cheek, brushed her lips with his. "Hmm," he said, after a minute. "Let's go upstairs. My room or yours?"

"I'm not sure. Let's try them both out."

CHAPTER 5

They ended the evening in Zach's room. Afterward, Keera stared at the ceiling for a dark hour while he slept. Their lovemaking, slow and exploratory at first, had grown more feverish within minutes. As if they had little time left together, each second precious, each one to be savored to its fullest. Best not to dwell about that.

She was sure they had connected in a previous life, not just the once either. Their bond was too fixed to have been forged in just this lifetime. But she'd never explored this, never tried to astral back to their earlier lives to confirm it. It might alter her view of him now, and the present mattered more than the past.

Keera rose and padded to her room. Stretched out on her bed. "Bardo? Can you take me to Dmitri? Show me the way he was."

She lay still for minutes, tamping down thoughts, waiting for the vibrations to start. If Bardo was willing. She didn't need him for this, but he sure expedited matters if he wanted to. Without him, she would flounder between time period searching for Dmitri, preferably at his most unlawful. The moment he was desperate to keep from the rest of the world. The critical fact that they could use against him.

The trembling, the vibrations along her spine announced her imminent move out of her body. A ripping sensation signaled her breaking through the membrane o the ordinary world, and within seconds, the darkness lifted reveal light and form.

This landscape she knew: East Coast city streets, not Manhattan where she'd spent several years, but Brooklyn. A beach off to her right, small waves, and she recognized it: Brighton Beach. The rides and stalls of Coney Island closed for the winter.

She searched for a clue to determine the year. Cars, plenty of cars, in the streets, but they gave her nothing. She'd never taken much notice of models or years of manufacture. All of these were old styles, but many were shiny and cared for, like new or nearly so.

People hurried past, oblivious to her presence on the sidewalk. No obvious clues in their dress either. A mix of retro and classic. Which was a clue in itself. Not the seventies or eighties with their clear and widely adopted, clothes and hairstyles. She was in the nineties or later.

Keera floated through cafes, not knowing what Dmitri looked like, but holding on to the certainty that once in his presence, she'd know him.

Then she was in a car, back seat, beside a tall Russian, dark hair, curling over his collar, dark hairs on the back of his fingers that wrapped around a revolver. Not the kind dragged out of holsters under jackets, but a monster of metal and death. An elongated barrel, the length of a forearm, resting on the window ledge, the car slowing behind a lone pedestrian strolling along the sidewalk.

The window slid down, the barrel emerging further into the daylight, and swiveling toward its strolling target. Dmitri, she now knew this, steadied his aim with both hands as the car drew level, and fired three soundless shots in quick succession. The gun bucked in his hand; incendiary particles flew out the barrel. His target shuffled sideways and dropped to the ground like a pile of discarded clothes.

People ran from the body, the gunshots, some with mouths open, but still no sounds. One person, frozen in place at first, made a tentative step towards the body before the car accelerated and she lost sight of him.

Dmitri gesticulated madly, shouting at the driver, but she couldn't hear him either. Bardo's way of protecting her from the trauma of witnessing a close-range killing. Stripping away all sound, protecting her from the emotional shock that might have flung her back to her body shaken and distressed.

She had witnessed Dmitri kill somebody—a rival, an enemy? A cold-blooded execution. Who died, and why? And when?

In answer, she found herself in somebody's apartment. Dmitri and the other man from the car, waiting, drinking. Yuri, a much younger Yuri, appeared. No buzzer, no door knock, Yuri was simply there. Time had shifted and she couldn't tell how much.

The men are laughing, fist-bumping like young dudes, but again she couldn't hear their conversation.

"I want to listen to them, Bardo," she said.

"It's not necessary," he replied, appearing beside her. "They're cheerful because they have removed a former colleague who had become a potential rival, that's all."

"That's all? Somebody just got killed, and you dismiss it so easily?"

"It was a quick passing. He wasn't much of an asset to the material world in any case. He'd already wasted his talents on empty pursuits. It was his time."

Bardo's detachment from the real world, her real world, always surprised her. The way he put it was that people only came into physical being to achieve particular outcomes during their lives. If they failed to do this, they returned until they got it right. It sounded fine as a philosophy, chilling to view in action.

"But still," she said, "why kill him? It's not the only way."

"Death is their preferred solution to any problem. You should be aware of this."

"Thanks. With every warning, I become even more dispirited. Can I assume that Dmitri was never charged with the killing?"

"Correct. The police had little interest in criminals eliminating each other. The investigation was cursory. No one talked. The case set aside."

"What year is this?"

"It's ten years ago by your date system, the Gregorian calendar. A useful measure of time, if you have to have one."

Keera watched the men refill shot glasses and toast each other like they'd won a major victory. Leaving a man dying on a sidewalk wasn't a cause for joy, at least not to her.

"Do you want to meet him?"

"Who?"

"Mikhail, the man you saw die."

"What!"

"He's the key to the issues you face. A little understanding will go a long way."

She didn't get a chance to agree. Before her, a man-shape filled out and became semi-solid. Stocky, that's all she could see. The rest of him was too dark and amorphous to make out. Only his vibration was detectable, and it was agitated. She waited for him to communicate.

"You saw what they did," the man-shape said.

She nodded.

"They care for nothing but themselves."

"You were one of them once," she said.

"Death changed me. The stupidity, the futility of that life became clear."

"What do you want of me?"

"My daughter is coming to you. You must help her."

"To keep her away from Dmitri?"

"No, to avenge me."

Mikhail's shape flexed, ballooning out in emphasis as he spoke. Despite his earlier words, it didn't sound like he had abandoned all earthly views.

"I won't be involved in a killing. Not in any way."

"You help her at the right time; that's all I ask."

Mikhail vanished faster than he had arrived, and before she could ask Bardo for any clarification, she woke up in her body.

She opened her eyes. Took a series of long, slow breaths to remove the sticky tension she'd carried back. She sat up slowly and saw Bardo alongside her, comfortable in a chair.

"How's this thing with Mikhail going to work out?" she asked. "I don't even understand what I'm supposed to do."

"You ever notice how the future becomes clearer the closer it is?"

"Please, no homilies. How will this daughter get involved?"

"Whatever will be, will be."

Keera rubbed her hands over her face. "Do you know how sick I am of hearing advice that makes no sense."

"It's the way it's meant to be."

"You could make it easier."

"A parent could do all her child's homework, too. Would that have the desired result?"

"Would it hurt you to give me some direct help now and then?"

Bardo smiled, cheerful as a card player holding the perfect hand. "Well, it'd hurt *you*. There's no gain being the passive recipient of others' long-term help. Some things you have to do for yourself."

It was no good arguing with Bardo. He had all the answers that somebody several centuries older than herself should.

"It'll all be over in a week," he said, unexpectedly.

"We'll be rid of these parasites?" Her spirit rising at the news.

"It'll end the way it's meant to end."

Sweet Jesus, Bardo was back to his obfuscatory best. She tried another tack. "Will Zach discover anything useful about Dmitri?"

"Wherever Zach's investigations take him, there'll be unintended consequences."

"Which means?"

"You can't poke a hornet's nest without risking stings."

Back to the homilies. Bardo wasn't surrendering any information she wanted. Why had he appeared then? This kind of debate they could have any time. Indeed, had had many times before.

She opened her mouth to protest more, but Bardo was gone.

His abrupt departure didn't signify any displeasure on his part. He never showed irritation or anger; his constant demeanor was one of genial conviviality.

This time, it was a signal that she wouldn't get any more information tonight. She must be asking the wrong questions. Damn.

Keera lay back and drew the bedcovers to her chin. Thought about rejoining Zach in the next room. But he wouldn't wake for hours, and she needed time to dispel the horrors that still clung to her.

To sleep, best not to dream.

CHAPTER 6

She was finishing her yogurt when Zach ambled in. Tousled and cheerful, he slid into the chair opposite her. "When did you wake up?" he asked.

"Hours ago. I tried to find Dmitri."

"Any luck?" He eyed her empty bowl with mild disgust and moved to forage in the fridge.

"I watched him gun down a man. Somewhere in Brooklyn. Years ago."

Zach straightened. "Jesus." He returned to his seat. "And?"

"Dmitri executed if that's the word, a former colleague."

He reached over and took her hands. "You okay?"

"Better than I was. It wasn't a fun night out."

"It must have been tough watching a killing."

"Bardo protected me, cut me off from the sounds, the smells. I couldn't pick up emotions. I was in the middle of it, but viewing it as a silent movie. Thank God."

Zach patted a hand and returned to the fridge. "You discover anything we can use on Dmitri? Like, is he breaking parole?"

"He got away with it. No arrest, no prison time."

Zach cracked a couple of eggs into a pan, organized coffee in a French press. "So, we have a cold case to investigate. You go back, find the missing evidence, and present it to the cops. *Voila*, Dmitri gone."

"What do you think I can do?" He still didn't understand how she worked. "I'm not a spy satellite. I gather short visions, a fragment of other lives. I'm not capable of a forensic exploration of the area or the time. I have to rely on what others show me."

"Your guide?"

"Not only him. Other beings often appear."

"Like who?" Zach carried his coffee and scrambled eggs to the table.

"Like Mikhail."

"Who's he?"

"The man Dmitri killed."

"He talked to you?"

"He did."

Zach smiled, pleased. "How about that. We have the victim who can lead us to the vital clue that gets Dmitri thrown into a concrete box."

"We have something. Let's not start assuming fantasies will come true."

"Yeah, but—"

"We have no proof. All we have is my tale, which isn't credible to any police force."

"Look. I know people in the Russian newspaper business," he said. "I should be able to contact somebody who's from that time. And from New York. The Russian emigres were fewer back then. Most everyone knew everyone else. I might link Dmitri to this unsolved crime."

"If we have six months. Which we don't."

Zach pushed scrambled egg clumps around his plate. "I understand how this works. You've told me yourself many times. You're only ever shown stuff for a reason. It's clear we're meant to find the evidence to nail Dmitri."

"I don't think that'll happen."

"Why not?"

"Mikhail had a daughter. She's alive, and coming here."

"To help us?"

"No. To kill Dmitri."

"The way it looks," Zach said as he rinsed the French press and wedged it into the dishwasher, "is we dig up what we can on Dmitri, I run it in the *Post*, and our nasty friend decides he hates the limelight and leaves us alone."

"More likely," Keera said, "he'll be so furious at what you've done, that he'll shoot you several dozen times."

"In my experience, all forms of lowlife hate the bright lights of exposure. They scuttle for cover because they do their best work in the dark. Killing me would only intensify the investigation against them."

"That sounds so righteous, except for one thing: these are not politicians caught with their hands in the wrong pocket. I'm amazed you expect these people to act rationally after you've seen firsthand they don't."

She was wrong. He wasn't expecting; he was hoping. The situation was a violent chemical reaction: a roiling mix of greed, revenge, and extortion. Impossible to control. The only way forward was to find something to stop these natural forces at work. Fear was the best.

"Let's see if we can expose something they don't want anybody to know about," he said. "Before they figure out where we are, and come after us again."

"You think that'll work?"

"I don't know. If we have a plan and it's crap, we dump it, and figure out another one. Without a plan,we can only react to whatever they dish up. I'm not sure about you, but my personality type doesn't allow me to do that."

"Zach, your personality type has yet to be recognized and categorized. Let's hope it stays that way. The world isn't ready for a whole bunch of you."

Howard called Zach around noon. "Here's a name for you," he said. "Dmitri Nikolai Rudin. Arrived in the U.S. in the early nineties. Entry port: Boston. Known to the FBI, but never brought in for questioning. Not by them or by any local police force. Mixing in shady émigré circles is his primary occupation. Sound like your man?"

"That description matches nearly every Russian I've met so far."

"You should try spending time with more respectable members of society."

"I can't. I'm a reporter. Can you get a photograph of this guy?"

"It'll cost extra."

"My line of credit's good for a few more pennies."

"I'll text the pic when it comes," Howard said and disconnected.

Howard's hacker pal was good, but not as good as Keera.

Given more time, she would discover the same information, and much more. Still, separate confirmation was helpful.

He called the only Russian reporter he knew in Chicago.

"Vlad, it's Zach. How's it going?"

"Don't you owe me a top whisky? I recall promises made."

The whisky was in payment for Vlad suggesting Sidirov as a useful contact. "Just checking your preferences. Also, I have another question."

"Sullivans Cove Single Malt. From Tasmania. What's your question?"

"I'd like to talk to any sensible Russian émigré who may have been in New York in the nineties. I want to get a feel for the time and place. You in touch with anybody like that? Someone doesn't carry a weapon, and doesn't want to extort money from me?"

"You mix with such terrible people," Vlad said.

Another one with helpful views. "I'm working on something, and it started in New York a couple of decades ago."

"You might get lucky with this old guy: Peter Yolkov. Freelancer, lives here in Chicago, but used to be based in Brooklyn.Doesn't put out much stuff these days." Vlad read off a number.

"Thanks. Anything else I should know?"

"I'll need a chaser to go with the whiskey. Maybe one of those fancy decanters, too."

"And I'll need a second job to pay for your information."

Zach called the number Vlad had given him.

"*Da?*"

"This is Zach Bones from the *Chicago Post*. Is this Peter Yolkov?"

"*Da.*"

The guy was a master of the monosyllable. "I'm hoping to get background on Russian émigrés to the U.S., New York in particular. Vlad Lebedev suggested you could help."

"Help? What kind of story are you doing? More crap about organized crime taking over this country?" His voice rose scornfully. "Well, it's true. End of story. You can have that for free."

"Nothing like that. More a look at how the best and brightest of them have fared since arriving. I want to compare examples in New York and Chicago. Vlad thought you'd know quite a few."

"You doing a story on New York Russians for a Chicago paper? You want me to believe this?"

"Okay, it's a complex story. Some New York guys are involved. I'm hoping you might know them."

"Who?"

Back to monosyllables. "Gennardy Sidirov."

"Stinking polecat. I know him, and it embarrasses me to admit it. That's it? One guy?"

"Dmitri Rudin." Crossed fingers it was the right Dmitri.

"Ah."

"You can help, then?"

Yolkov breathed noisily into his mouthpiece, probably sorting out angles and rewards. He came up with one. "Why don't you buy me lunch?" he said. "You get hour of my time. Today is good. In two hours."

Zach was checking the location of Yolkov's restaurant of choice on his cell when he noticed Keera staring at him quizzically, waiting to be filled in.

"I have someone who knows Dmitri," he said. "I'm meeting him for lunch. Gotta prepare my questions."

Keera inspected him for a moment. "I sense that it's not presenting as a dangerous situation. I also sense you'd go even if it were."

"Any information we get on Dmitri is gold. It's only lunch, not far from here. I'll be back in a few hours."

"I know," she said. "No one will hit you either."

"You're so sure I'll be safe. Why can't you get the same warnings for yourself?"

"It doesn't work like that; I've told you. Psychics can't be reliably psychic about themselves. It's part of the deal."

"I'll take a cab."

She pursed her lips.

"I know, I know," he said. "I'll stop a few blocks before the restaurant. Walk the rest of the way. But I don't figure anyone's watching. They couldn't have heard of this meet yet."

"Keep that thought close, Zach. You're betting your freedom on it."

CHAPTER 7

Keera opened the garage doors and backed her father's Mercedes into the driveway. She drove to a supermarket to stock up with fresh food. Otherwise, they would spend the week living off chips and beer and wine and cheese.

She added a case of beer for the old guys behind Grinders and drove over. The brand the guys had mentioned had slipped her mind. "What's popular?" she asked a guy nearby and waved at the display of cans.

"Me, I like the mountain freshness of Coors," he replied. She dragged a case onto her cart.

The two old guys were waiting, leaning against a wall, but straightened when they recognized her.

"These guys came. We told them we saw nobody," said the guy who'd spoken yesterday. He glanced at his buddy. "We thought you weren't coming back. The kid inside knew nothing about this deal."

"Life got in the way." Keera popped the trunk and pointed to the case. "I forgot what you asked for, my mind was a bit fuzzy at the time, so I hope you like Coors. I'm not familiar with beer brands."

He lifted the case out. "You drink enough of them, you stop caring about the differences." He staggered back to the wall, probably their main hango'ut, and expertly tore the flaps open. Handed a can to his pal, popped the top of his own, and held it up in salute.

"I have to go inside for a minute," Keera said. "Watch the car, will you?"

They both nodded.

Josh wasn't inside, but the female barista knew her and held up her pack.

"Thanks, Tori," Keera said. "Tell Josh I owe him a favor."

"I heard it was a bit freaky yesterday," Tori said. "Guys muscling in here, looking for you."

"Josh okay?"

"Yeah. He said you were out the back, and you know what? They actually opened the door to the ladies' restroom. After that, they looked all over the place for you, even checked under the tables. Two of them ran out to the back, but I guess you were gone. Who were they?"

"Not the most friendly of people."

Tori waited for Keera to expand further, but Keera turned to go. "I have to run. I'll catch up with Josh later."

That was a straight-out lie. It was risky even coming here today; she wouldn't come back until these new Russians were out of her life. And she had no timeframe for that.

Outside, the two drinkers had already dropped a couple of empties each and had grown more cheerful with their third can.

"Please don't litter," she said as nicely as she could.

The two scrambled to collect the empties and made a show of dropping them into a dumpster.

"Thanks again," she said, waggling fingers, as she put the car in gear and headed for home.

A couple of miles along, Bardo changed her plans.

Take a left here.

Keera took the next left.

Ahead, a crowd had gathered outside a shopfront. Medics leaned over a body in the doorway; uniformed police watched onlookers pressing against the warning tape.

She pulled over to the curb and approached the crowd, car keys in hand. The body, stretched out on the ground, wore the shabby shoes of the homeless. Keera scanned the crowd for any sign of the dead man's spirit body. A violent end often meant that a soul lingered, shocked and uncertain of its state.

She mentally checked off the bystanders, noting those still in the physical world. Sometimes it was hard to separate the dead from the living; both appeared solid at first glance. Often, the only clue was a faint shimmer around the outline of a body. The dead were easiest to spot when they behaved differently from the living. Like floating a few inches offthe ground.

A disturbed, restless figure hovered near a pair of detectives examining the body. Hovered, as in a foot off the ground. The detectives ignored him, even though he was inside the tape because he was invisible to them. He talked excitedly, waving his hands for emphasis. He hadn't yet realized he now existed on a different energy plane from the living, separated by elemental barriers. For the detectives, he simply didn't exist.

Keera called out silently to the man. "They can't see you."

He turned toward her. "You can?"

"Of course." Their exchange was inaudible on the physical plane. "If you have something important to tell them," she said, "I might be able to pass it on."

Just maybe. Not very likely. Cops tended to dismiss psychics who came forward with "special" information. They were naturally skeptical of anything illogical—and because ninety-nine percent of psychics handed over random impressions that led nowhere. A total waste of everybody's time.

He drifted closer. He owned a fifty-year-old face but street people aged fast. Spiky hair topped crumpled clothes, and he stared at her as if she made no sense. All the while he twisted a plain ring on his finger. "He took the ring. It's here, but not on my other body. How's that happen?"

"The physical ring's one, but your memory of it stays. To you, it's solid, right?" The spirit ring gleamed silver, a faint trace of filigree as its only decoration.

He didn't answer, twisted the ring around and around. "I have to find it."

"You have all you need—your soul," she said. "You can't take material things with you." The man lived on the street, owned nothing much of value, and still he wanted to keep what he had. She couldn't explain that he was now free of all physical possessions if he wanted to be.

Some people were very bound to their stuff; they refused to leave them, even at death. If he was one of those, he was doomed to a restless afterlife. Not a great place to spend eternity.

Keera understood now—this was why Bardo had steered her here. To carry out a rescue mission, to smooth this man's path to the next level.

"He walked up," the man said. "Grabbed my hand, tried to

yank the ring off. I was kinda out of it, didn't react fast enough. Clenched my fist so he couldn't snatch my ring but he whacked me across the head." He ran his fingers along a temple as if searching for a tender spot. Of course, it didn't exist in a spirit.

"Next thing, I'm standing next to my body and this jerk is walking away... with my ring. I chased him, but it was like I wasn't there. I couldn't grab him. Nothing." He held out his hand. "Donnie's the name."

Keera ignored the proffered hand; shaking hands made no sense if you had no body. Donnie hadn't yet realized he could alter his appearance just by thinking it. Once he figured that out, he'd revert to a younger, more attractive version of himself. All the dead people she knew had adjusted like this. Pretty quickly, too.

"Best not mingle our energies," she said. "You think he killed you?"

Donnie shook his head. "I'm not dead, just outta my head. Some killer weed, though. I've never been like, buzzed in this way. I mean, I see myself from the outside. How freaky is that? Gotta get some more."

This was not going to be a smooth transition for Donnie. The most problems Keera had encountered in the past were with the elderly. They had often spent their last days in various stages of dementia, and found the afterlife no more confusing than their previous one. Some proved impossible to convince that they were dead, and they remained in their old homes, bothering, sometimes terrifying the new occupants. A major stoner like Donnie wasn't going to be easy work. Thanks, Bardo.

It won't take long, you've done rescues before.

Yes, she replied, but aren't there more important things I

should be dealing with right now?

From your position, it's difficult to see what's important and what isn't.

You know, right now I'm involved in a life and death situation.

So is Donnie.

There was no winning this argument. Bardo was gently bullying her into fulfilling one of the obligations that come with being a medium— assisting the newly dead.

"Who are you?" Donnie asked.

Good question. What could she tell him that he could grasp?

"Like, how come you can see me and hear me?" He waved his arms at the onlookers. "But everybody else here ignores me."

Best to start with the truth. It might work. "They ignore you because you're dead. I see you because I sometimes see dead people."

He laughed. "You're funny."

The truth was useless for the moment. Maybe humoring him while he figured it out for himself was a better plan. "The person who took the ring. What did he look like?" The small crowd around them gave no clues—no killing vibe, no giveaway inner turmoil that telegraphed spinning emotions. Curiosity and fear of death were the most common reactions. The killer had left the scene.

"Young guy, well, younger than me," Donnie said. "Dark hair, hoodie, a dumbshit tatt on his neck. I have to find my ring."

He was going to drive her crazy with that ring. She tried the truth again. "It's like this, Donnie. If you find it, you can't do anything with it. You can't move it; you can't take it back. All you can do is look at it; you can't even touch it."

"I don't know what you're talking about, and I don't wanna know." Defiance creeping into his voice.

"You have no physical body anymore, got it?" If this guy stayed stupid, she was going to give up and go home. You can't help those who can't be helped.

"Seems like I got two bodies," Donnie said. "One over there and one I can feel."

"You don't think that's strange?"

"It's amazing weed, is what it is. I told you. This dude handed me a totally righteous blunt. Had a time with it, and it feels like I'm still having a time with it."

"For God's sake, Donnie. You. Are. Dead."

"I. Am. Not."

Donnie was seriously irritating. Words would never sway him. Time to show him, not tell him. "I'm going home," she said. "I live a few blocks from here. Give me time to organize myself, and I'll rejoin you. On your level."

"You should score some of that weed yourself. It's major league stuff."

She wanted to slap him sensible. "No weed can help me. I can join you on your level briefly, that's all, but it should be enough time."

"To do what?"

"To show you what you need to see."

Donnie's attention wandered to his body and came back to her. "Where should I wait?"

Keera jingled her car keys. "Wait wherever you want. I'll find you, I'll find your ring and you, you'll find that you're wrong. Dead wrong."

CHAPTER 8

Shaggy silver hair flopped over his ears and collar, half-obscuring the button eyes of a dollar-store teddy bear; his windcheater was a twenty-year survivor of wardrobe favoritism, and his face was a cross-lined map of two unfortunate past habits: smoking and drinking—both excessive.

He rose, offered Zach his hand, a no-nonsense grip, and waved him to the chair across the table. The restaurant was painted burgundy throughout, except for a lone, exposed brick wall. The furniture matched.

The lighting fixtures weren't as coordinated. They came from every decade of the past century. Prints decorated the walls; prints of people looking like they had stepped out of War and Peace, or out of a charity store.

"What's this crap story?" Yolkov asked as a pleasant starter. "I looked in your *Post* today, found nothing with your byline."

"I don't get published every day," Zach said. "I have room to follow my stories."

"You got ID?"

Zach slid his press pass across the table. Yolkov perused it, handed it back.

"You think I have story for you?" he asked.

"I'm interested in Dmitri Rudin," Zach said as the waitress arrived.

Yolkov didn't check the menu. "Salted herring with vegetables for both of us. And three Baltika Dark."

The waitress scribbled on her pad, raised an eyebrow at Zach.

"I guess so," he said. He'd warmed to many Russian dish he tried except for blinis. This seemed a good time to try something else. Why three beers?

"Rudin's an nimal," Yolkov said. As the waitress walked away, he checked her ass. "Stay away from him."

"What about Yuri Buteyko? You know him?"

"That fussy little shit? FSB, why they took him in, who knows? But he was good with contacts back in old country. So Rudin looked after him. He's doing time somewhere."

"Arizona. Killed one of his Russian pals."

"Never trust little guy. They dream big." Yolkov patted his pockets, looking for cigarettes, then stopped. "Why did American government fuck up a good country with no-smoking laws?"

"It's called health. They have that in Russia?"

Yolkov dismissed the thought with a wave. "We don't care about health, we prefer to live life."

Let any Russian start discussing the merits of American lifestyles versus Russian ones and they'd be there until midnight. Zach steered the conversation back to Dmitri.

"This Rudin," he said. "I hear he was involved in a shooting of a fellow Russian in Brooklyn a few years ago."

Yolkov gave him a tight smile. "You're wading into a swamp,

Mr. Reporter. Rudin's tied to a string of unfortunate deaths. Which one?"

"A drive-by. Ten years ago."

The waitress brought their plates and beers. Placed them roughly on the table, as if it were an insult to serve people, and stalked away.

"Is she angry with you or me?" Zach asked, eyeing the fish covered in layers of boiled and grated vegetables. He picked up the dark beer and started on it. All beer was fine. Anytime. This one was no exception.

"She's angry with herself. Figured she'd be a movie star by now. Sure has ass for it."

An ass Yolkov might have groped a couple of times, Zach realized, which explained the high-class service. "Are you married?" he asked. Made it sound conversational and relaxed. Like he was interested in Yolkov's personal life.

"No more."

"You like the experience?"

"I like dining with someone, not counting this moment, I like arguing with another person instead of just myself, and I like spooning at night. Also, other matters that are best carried out in darkness." Yolkov swallowed more beer and contemplated an interior vista he wouldn't share with anybody.

"You dating anybody?"

Yolkov glared at him. "You tried it recently? You ask a woman question, and they frown at phone before they answer you."

"What kind of questions do you ask?"

"Simple things. Like, what is the true origin of universe?"

"Who were you dating—Einstein's grandniece?"

"It's not a real question, it's a conversation starter, and they cannot manage it."

"The drive-by," Zach said. "What can you tell me?"

Yolkov drained half of a bottle. Waited a second or two to run his tongue over his lips then drained the other half. Put it down, pushed it away, drew the third bottle closer.

"He did it, no question. Did cops care? No. Russians killing Russians was not a priority for them."

"How do you know it was him?" Zach asked.

"Driver drank with me once, got talkative."

"You publish anything about it?"

"Would I be sitting here if I had?"

Zach forked into the dish and sampled a taste. Not bad, if you were hungry after sending wretched citizens to the gulags all day.

"What was the killing about?" he asked.

"Money, what else?"

Yolkov worked through his food like he was harvesting crops before early rains came.

"What was the victim's name?"

He shrugged. "Who cares? So long ago, I can't remember."

He hardly paused the flow of food from plate to mouth, but he had to be lying. No journalist ever forgot a name or the whole story that went with the name. Best remembered were the parts that couldn't be published for legal reasons, or because the pressure from powerful quarters became too great to resist.

Not being able to tell the whole story was a frequent and painful part of the profession. Few journalists resisted the chance to spill the unpublished stuff at any opportunity. Especially to other sympathetic journalists.

Yolkov was lying.

Time to help his memory.

Zach said, "The victim's name, it wouldn't be Mikhail by any chance?"

That stopped the food train. Yolkov pushed his plate away and swallowed more beer. "You're ruining good lunch, reporter boy."

"Sorry, it goes with the job. Who was this Mikhail?"

"An associate of Rudin's. They fell out. That's not a smart career move where Rudin's concerned."

"So, Rudin had him gunned down?"

Yolkov responded with raspy noises that Zach interpreted as a chuckle. "No, Mr. Reporter. Rudin enjoys close-up stuff himself. He wouldn't farm out the most rewarding moments of his career."

"Isn't it more normal for the guy at the top to distance himself from the actual crimes? To give him convincing deniability."

"That's only if you have police system that works as intended, more or less." He waggled a hand. "Now, Russia is in the hands of factional interests, who act like a mafia but control state. This is nothing new; the Soviets perfected this system, as did the Romans before them. But now Russians are allowed to travel. The fields of America glow much greener than those in Russia."

"Rudin finds it easier to operate here?"

"Absolutely. The police here are only beginning to adjust to this kind of criminal, but they're a long way behind. They assume mafias operate like the established Italian ones. Russians don't build huge organizations — they keep them small, and they break up often; or you could say they stay small because they break up often. Either way, it's harder for police to eliminate a hundred small syndicates than a handful of large ones. Small groups form and spread faster than large ones. It'd be easier to empty the ocean of krill."

Yolkov resumed clearing his plate and emptying the second beer. He signaled the waitress by pointing to his and Zach's beers.

Zach asked, "What was Mikhail's last name?"

He smiled at Zach's admission he didn't know it. "I'm not telling you."

"But you could?"

"Of course, but it's safer for both of us that I don't."

"But I'll find out anyway. So why not tell me?"

Yolkov didn't reply, sat like a contemplative stone figure, smug, but inadvertently signaling to the whole world that he still retained an active interest in Rudin, and that this Mikhail was a vital part of it. He was so bad at lying that he couldn't even deceive somebody by staying silent.

Zach changed tack "What's Rudin's main line of interest?"

"What's in this for me?" Yolkov replied. "You've already got lunchtime's worth of information."

"You haven't told me much; your overview I could've read on Google. Any chance Rudin's involved in data theft?"

He laughed, leaned over and slapped Zach's shoulder. "You're first-class reporter, I can see that."

The waitress clunked two beers on the table and walked away. Left the dirty plates.

"These people," Yolkov said, pointing to the waitress with his chin. "They should never have been liberated from serfdom. They were surly slaves for centuries, and after a hundred years of freedom, they still act like surly slaves."

The guy was wasting time, hoping to exhaust Zach with

pointless asides. "Who does Rudin target?" Zach asked.

"Big store chains, government departments. He has a bunch of guys who have set up systems. These systems, all day, all night, probe any accessible servers searching for weakness. Once they find one, they break in and loot."

"What do they want?"

"What do you think? Identities, credit card details, bank account details, and, of course, passwords." Yolkov finished his beer and pointed at Zach's untouched second bottle.

"You have it," Zach said. "The alcohol content is high, and I need to keep a clear head today."

"You find alcohol alcoholic, do you? Well, that's God's plan, Mr. Reporter." He put the bottle to his lips.

Zach considered bringing up the daughter Keera had mentioned but decided against it. He didn't know much about her; hell, nothing except that she existed. An old hand like Yolkov would spot a fishing expedition immediately. It'd be smarter to save this snippet for another time. Yolkov might trust him more then.

Yolkov said, "You have more questions that have no answers?"

The Russian was getting philosophic, a bad sign, and his speech was slowing; it was time to wrap this up. Zach caught the waitress's eye and made a signing gesture on his palm.

"You're in hurry, Mr. Reporter," Yolkov said. "Or am I expensive source?"

"I've enjoyed this meeting. I'd like to do it again soon. How's that suit you?"

"You're okay for a cheapskate. But if you're investigating Dmitri Rudin, I won't see you as often as you think. You'll disappear like many before you."

"I won't do anything stupid."

"You won't have to. If he thinks you going to cause trouble, his data experts will find you anytime, anywhere you hide."

This wasn't good news. Could he trust Yolkov's information? Maybe Keera could find out. First step was to ascertain that this sodden example of the media wasn't secretly playing in Dmitri's band.

Yolkov regarded the five empties with mild irritation. As if he should have ordered a crate of beer at the start. He said, "One other thing about Dmitri Rudin. He's impossible to find."

"He's scooted back to Russia where he can buy off the law?"

"No. In Russia, you never sure who has power over you from one month to next. You don't know how much you will pay to stay in business. Here is much better: the cops are consistent, the honest ones stay honest, the corrupt ones stay reasonable. The rules are set after first transaction. He'll stay here unless he has to leave. Brooklyn is very comfortable place for homesick Russians." He reached for his cigarettes before stopping in frustration again.

Zach said, "Dmitri Rudin is not in Brooklyn; he's in Chicago."

Yolkov froze, only for a split second, but long enough to give away his reaction to anyone waiting for it. Whether he was surprised at the news or surprised that Zach knew it was impossible to judge.

"He prefers our weather?"

"I didn't ask him. The situation precluded small talk."

"You met him?"

"Please, I'm trying to forget that encounter."

Yolkov's eyes inched together as he processed this

information. "It's not a surprise, he's moved. He prefers place far from his enemies. In his line of work, he can base himself anywhere. His little army of techies works out of Russia. He doesn't have to. You have address?"

"Not yet."

"I'd be interested in it when you have it."

"You don't have much to swap."

"What I have, Mr. Reporter, is worth more than lousy lunch."

The waitress returned and dropped the check on the table. Left the dirty dishes again.

"Thanks for the information." Zach stood, picking up the check. "We should talk again. My interest in Rudin is more than passing, as you've guessed. It's in my interests that he's brought to account for his crimes. I'd appreciate any way you can help me."

"You're wanting to track him down?"

Raised eyebrows advertised Yolkov's bewilderment.

"And I'll succeed, don't worry."

"If you look for him, he'll know. He collects data you wouldn't believe you're generating."

"I move pretty fast if I have to."

Yolkov shook his shaggy head. "What I was saying earlier, Mr. Reporter, if Rudin wants to meet you, then you'll be kneeling at his feet a half-hour after he gets this notion."

CHAPTER 9

Zach scanned the street for a cab, batting away the anxiety clinging to him. What if Yolkov worked for Dmitri? Who knew what was true in their rat-eat-rat world? He might be calling him right now, saying the reporter is leaving the restaurant.

No, that didn't make sense. If Yolkov wanted to sell him out, he would've called Dmitri before the meet. Invited him to join them. With an assistant who'd stick the pointy end of an elbow up a pesky nose.

His cell burst into electronic beats. Howard.

"Are you considering coming in today?"

"Thought I might work from the comfort and safety of my home," he said.

Howard grunted. "I'm asking because my contact wants to meet you. He says that the places you're going with your questions are extremely sensitive. He'd like a face-to-face, to make sure you're not a disturbed person."

"Of course I'm disturbed, I work for a newspaper."

"I suspect you are, Zach. But notice how some of us still

maintain a grip on reality. It takes inner strength, that's all. My friend would like to meet you here today. Any time before the afternoon rush hour."

"I'm coming in."

A taxi came into view as he killed the call. "The *Chicago Post*," Zach said. "Rear entrance, the loading bays."

"No problem," the cabbie said. He merged with the traffic and cruised south. "You look pretty well dressed for a warehouse worker if you don't mind me saying so."

There had to be cab drivers in this town who liked to drive in silence. Zach hadn't met one yet. "Today I need to make a discreet entrance," he replied.

The cabbie laughed softly. "You a reporter that wrote something somebody don't like, and now you got a protest group out front?"

"I get that problem all the time. Today is special and private."

The cabbie stayed quiet until they neared the *Post* building. Quiet, but his jaw working like it had a lot more to say.

"Give me a guesstimate for the fare," Zach said. "I'll pay now,' cos I'll be moving fast when we get there."

"I'd say around eighty bucks oughta do it."

The meter showed nearly forty bucks. Two blocks to go. He couldn't afford to get out now, too far from safety. Zach dropped two fifties next to the driver. Being unfriendly was expensive these days.

"Have lunch on me," he said. Hope you choke on it.

The cabbie drew up outside the loading bay. Ahead, four cars down the street two men sat in a black BMW. They were already opening their doors. Zach threw open his and ran for the elevator.

"Have a nice day, ya hear?" the cabbie called after him.

The elevator doors were closing as he ran; he wouldn't make it in time. A quick look over his shoulder confirmed it. The two from the car were now running.

One man had exited the elevator, a building security guard, busy lighting up a cigarette.

Zach stopped in front of the guard and jerked his pass card out. "I'm authorized to be in this building," he rasped at him. "The two goons behind just tried to mug me."

The guard dropped a hand on his gun butt. The men stopped ten yards away.

"You two," the guard said, pointing at them, the cigarette between two fingers, "have no right to be here. You want to see somebody inside, you go through the front entrance."

The men didn't speak, considering their options, Zach guessed. The guard wasn't young and fit, looking for action, ready to practice his karate moves on anybody who invaded his space. Nothing like that. But he carried an air of assurance across his solid frame: an air that everything would work out the way he wanted. The kind of guy with an attitude you didn't want to fool with.

The men stayed where they were.

The guard said, "Up there, in the corner behind me, is a camera recording your not-so-handsome faces." He rested a hand on a radio receiver attached to his left shoulder. "I tap this button, and the superintendent calls the police." He blew smoke their way like he was fumigating the spot they stood in.

They looked at each other, and walked back to their car.

The elevator doors opened.

The guard said, "Here's your ride to safety."

"Thanks," Zach said. "I appreciate your help. My name's Zach Bones."

The guard offered a hand. "Ernie Suggs. I seen you coming and going at the front. Didn't expect to find you out here."

"You know how it is: some days, the whole world is against you the minute you get out of bed. Today called for extra discretion."

Ernie glanced over at the gates, the two goons no longer in sight. "I hate those types; they figure muscles and guns make everything right." He took a deep drag on his cigarette. "They only understand people who think the same way."

Security guards have lots of time to develop their philosophies, and Ernie had used his time diligently.

"I agree," Zach said. "Glad you convinced them to leave."

"It was well within my pay scale, and I enjoyed it."

Ernie stuck a foot in the elevator to hold the doors open for him. "Well, you have a nice day now, Mr. Bones."

He didn't prolong a faked friendly conversation like he was angling for a tip; Ernie seemed as straightforward as he sounded. The world needed more like him, but it would have to wait.

Once back in her room, Keera stretched out on her yoga mat, breathed in slowly and deeply, and waited for the roaring in her ears to signal the tearing apart of body and soul. Within minutes she slipped from her body and drifted through the ceiling into the night sky. To Donnie, she thought, and discovered herself on the fringe of onlookers at the crime scene again.

Donnie was hunched behind two detectives examining his

body. He was saying something to them again, still disbelieving that they couldn't hear him.

She joined him and said, "Why don't we just listen and see what they've found?"

"How old do you think he is, Gordo?" The female detective squatted alongside the body, her question directed at her colleague.

Gordo played a flashlight over the man's face and shrugged. "Probably a homeless case—smells like one. Could be forty, or fifty even. Let the ME make the call, huh?" He tracked the torch beam around the body. "The medics say he's got a head wound. Would have figured an overdose myself."

"He doesn't look like he could afford anything to get him through the night." She slipped on a pair of latex gloves and patted the body down, rummaged in pockets and retrieved a photograph. At one time it had been folded in half, a crinkled line ran across it but not enough to obscure an outdoor shot of a man and a woman. "Gimme more light, Gordo," she asked, and he brought the flashlight up closer.

"You reckon that's him?" he said.

The couple in a lovers' clinch, oblivious of the photographer, clutching each other like they'd finally found their soul mate after years of searching. The female flipped the photo. *Mez and me.* "They look so right together," she said softly.

"There's blood on the scalp," Gordo said, lifting the head. "More blood on the door frame." He played the beam back along the body's hands and bent closer. "The vic wore a ring, see the pale circle around the finger? Maybe he was killed for it."

"You saw that in this light?" the female said. "You're good."

Gordo straightened. "Wanted to be a doctor once. Ended up a

cop."

"No talent?"

"No money for med school. We're done for now. Tell 'em he's ready for the body bus."

The female detective said, "Maybe somebody robbed him while he was unconscious."

"Or hit him hard enough to kill him first," Gordo said.

Keera asked Donnie, "You getting a sense you're dead yet?"

CHAPTER 10

When Zach reached his desk, Howard was talking to a guy in a well-fitted dark suit, no tie, and a shirt with covered buttons.

"Zach," Howard said. "My friend I was telling you about. Royston Plenty. Zach Bones."

Plenty offered a quick grip. Smiled easy, floppy brown locks drooped over half his forehead.

"I understand you need help," he said, in a rounded English accent. Not the Queen's cut-glass version, but one of those cute ones you find when you drive out of London.

"I want information on a person and his whereabouts," Zach replied.

"My specialty. Can we talk somewhere private?"

Howard said, "Try the interview room."

Zach led the way, Plenty slinging a small pack over his right shoulder. The room was small but accommodated a table with room for six chairs. One window showed the world outside. Fake wood panels decorated the walls that displayed paintings of a world gone by. A contrast of sharp-edged concrete and weathered, tumbledown structures. Matched the way Zach looked, and felt.

"Nice," Plenty said, with cheerful insincerity. He pulled a black box the size of a fat smartphone from his pack. "Let's see if we have eavesdroppers." He pressed a switch and placed the box on the table. A solitary light glowed red. "We're not alone," he said.

"Somebody's listening to us?" Zach was astounded.

"Somebody's recording us, probably."

"The hell for?"

Plenty lifted a warning finger. Drew out another box similar to the first one and placed it alongside. Switched it on. A slight pulsating hum filled the room.

"Can you bear that sound? Some can't."

"I'm fine," Zach said.

"This sends out noise-canceling waves, among other things; any recording will be muffled. It's not perfect but at this preliminary stage, it'll do us."

"You expected this?"

"No, but it doesn't surprise me. The upper levels of management may want an early heads up if you're about to plunge the paper into the hottest of legal waters."

"They don't trust us?"

"They don't trust you to keep their financial investment front of mind. They may also shave old their souls to the NSA. Shall we move to the matter at hand?"

They settled in chairs and Zach said, "I'm looking for all the information you can get on a Dmitri Rudin. Russian emigre, spent a few years in Brooklyn, now believed to be living here. He keeps a Gennardy Sidorov, a Russian reporter, on side." He spelled out both names.

Plenty waited.

"You going to write this down?" Zach asked.

"The written word is a double-edged sword. I have an eidetic memory."

"Eidetic memory?"

"A photographic memory. Please continue."

"I understand that he's involved with data theft."

Plenty grinned. "What a surprise. It's the natural career choice of hundreds of Russians who arrived here after the fall of the Soviet Union, all claiming to be computer programmers. Their records were difficult to check, but they proved, for the most part, to be competent when employed."

"And they turned to crime?"

"Not all of them, no. But in Russia, if you don't game the system, you get left behind. It's a regular part of their life. The social systems set up here, and in Europe, assume a more honest population. We're easy pickings."

Zach recalled Yolkov's remark about not needing to live in the US to steal data. "Can't they do their thieving from Russia?"

"They can and do, but they need somebody on the ground here to identify the best targets. Chain stores with their credit card systems, government departments with personal records, that kind of thing. The guys dancing their fingers over the keyboards can be anywhere, yes."

Plenty waited for the next question while Zach tried to figure out what it would be.

"You're a Brit, right?" he said. "But you have contacts in US law enforcement, correct?"

"I can't reveal the nature of any if any, contacts." He smiled back. "It's part of the business plan."

"How do you know Howard?"

"We were college friends. I completed a PPE degree at Oxford, then came here for further study."

"PPE?"

"Politics, Philosophy, and Economics. The degree you do when you don't know what to do with your life."

"Useful?"

"In ways you can't imagine."

"How did you get into this electronic surveillance business?"

Plenty spread his hands apart. "I thought I came here to listen to your story, not the other way around."

"It'll help me to understand your background. Make me more comfortable working with you."

Plenty hunched forward over the table like he was about to divulge precious personal secrets. An old technique that made Zach smile.

"I've always had an interest in electronics," he said. "One day a friend complained that his business rivals often seemed to predict his next move. I knew enough to neutralize the bugs I found in his office. His kind words about me spread, and more work followed. Soon, it was necessary to learn computer coding to keep abreast of technology. I discovered I was quite adept at it. It was just another language to me, and I was already fluent in several European languages. But I collected too many clients to handle."

"How did you solve that problem?"

"This is where the economics part of my degree came in useful: I charged more than I thought I was worth. Only half of my clients dropped me. I now have a wonderful work/life balance. They say money doesn't make you happy, but I've found that it certainly ameliorates a shitload of discomforts."

Zach leaned back. "What you're saying is that you're too expensive for what you do."

"Oh no. Too expensive for some, that's all. You want cheap,? Find a high-school coder who can hack a Facebook account, insert fake posts. See if that solves your problems."

Plenty wasn't offended; he remained at ease with the blunt questioning, and the implied insult he was a huckster. This was encouraging. Zach didn't need a precious nerdy operator who got huffy when cross-examined.

But the back story the guy was offering? Total garbage. Unless everybody in the UK relied on old school friends to carry out expert debugging. Pals with no formal training in that field weren't the best option when a business had a serious and illegal bugging problem to solve.

"You know something," Zach said. "I don't believe any of your story."

Plenty smiled again. He sure knew how to handle insults. "Of course you don't. What kind of journalist would you be if you swallowed the first story presented to you?"

"You start every relationship with a new client by lying to him?"

"I could give you another tale that would survive even protracted checking, but why should I? Most clients don't care about my past, especially after they see the results."

"But I do."

"Only because you think that if you know more about me, we exchange personal stories, we'll become friends." Plenty spread his hands again in rueful acknowledgment of some truth. "It's so American to want to be friends with people you employ. It's a middle-class thing, a way of demonstrating that you're classless. But it's unnecessary with me. I don't want to be your friend, although I'm sure you'd be a solid pal, convivial company and all that. I only want to complete the project I'm hired for, as efficiently as possible. Does that make sense to you?"

Despite his apparent professorial detachment, Plenty appeared to carry his own baggage about class. And it was just as hard to believe this new Plenty as the old one. He was also deliberately revealing personal views, which may or may not be true, to draw Zach into a false sense of companionship. This trick Zach had used himself often enough to vouch for its effectiveness. You reveal more when you feel safe.

Plenty could be as good as Howard had said, but he'd need watching. It wasn't necessary to mention the money at this stage, if ever. The guy would probably double his fee if he found out. Let him believe that he was involved in a mere journalist's story hunt.

"Okay," Zach said. "Let's start with this Dmitri Rudin. I heard that he was connected to a fatal shooting of a fellow Russian in Brooklyn. Ten years ago. It'd be helpful if I knew what the local authorities have on him."

"Ten years ago?"

"Maybe a little longer. Is that time frame too broad?"

"Once I have the right identity, time is immaterial. Computers make wonderful time travelers. They will retrieve your past life anytime you want."

"While you're at it, can you search for a Peter Yolkov, once of Brooklyn but who lives here now. Y.O.L.K.O.V. A Russian reporter. Knows of Rudin, knows more than he's telling me."

"What's your interest in Rudin?"

"If you're so good, you'll find out."

Plenty burst into laughter. "As long as your interest is legal, I don't have a problem." He cocked his head. "You were puffed when you came in. Did you jog here in your work clothes?"

"I needed to sprint when a couple of Dmitri's goons spotted me outside." They would still be out there, he realized, with another team out the front.

"And they're waiting for you to come out again?" Plenty was ahead of him.

"I guess. Can you suggest evasion tactics?"

He shut down his devices and zipped them up in his pack. "Personal security is not my usual field, but let me make a call when we get out of this room." He pulled a business card from a pocket. "Send a thousand dollars to that email, and I'll start right away."

"A thousand?"

"That buys you two hours, which might be all you need."

"A thousand? You need another shirt, or what?"

Plenty rose to his feet. "Quality is never cheap, Mr. Bones. Speed is also expensive."

"Yeah, but..."

"If I discover more than expected, I'll advise you, and you can decide whether you want me to follow up on the new information."

"And you get paid by email? That's hardly secretive."

"Mr. Bones, my work is, of course, confidential, but my income is an open book to the IRS. Those people can give me headaches I don't need."

Zach inspected the card. No name, just a generic email

address, and a phone number.

"The phone number," Plenty said, "is good for one week only. If this arrangement continues past that time, the number dies, and I'll give you another one."

Back in the main office Plenty called somebody, murmured into his cell and said, "Hold on a minute, will you?" He turned to Zach. "A half-hour diversion to stop the watchers will cost you seven-fifty." His raised eyebrow implied that it might be a high price for a lowly reporter. He wasn't wrong.

"Seven fifty?"

"Plus tax."

"Tax?"

"These guys are totally legit," Plenty said. "They obey all laws."

"How do they describe their business?"

"Oh, just transportation facilitation services, I assume. Yes or no?"

At this rate, the three million in the Caymans would be gone before he could give it away.

"Okay," he said. "I'll try to sneak it through my expenses." Best to let Plenty believe it was the *Post*'s money, not his.

"Add it to my payment," Plenty said. "I'll disclose a personal interest: I get a small commission. Tell me about the watchers."

When Plenty's cell beeped twice, minutes later, they rode a rear elevator down.

"When the doors open, walk fast to the waiting cab," Plenty said.

"A cab?"

"With respect, Mr. Bones, I don't believe the *Post* would spring for a limo or a highly modified escape vehicle."

"Yeah, but a cruddy cab? For all those bucks?"

"Evasion's a process of disappearing. A cab is fine today."

They stepped out into the loading bays, a yellow cab waiting, back doors open. Plenty pushed Zach in ahead of him, but not before Zach saw the BMW flash indicators prior to moving out on the road.

He twisted in his seat to watch the Russians follow, but they never got the chance. A rattly, rusted truck, loaded with wooden pallets and crates, pulled up alongside the BMW as it began to move out. It pulled up close enough to scrape paint and hem the car in. The car jerked to a halt. A window wound down, and an arm with a fist banged on the side of the truck. Whatever happened after that, Zach didn't see; the cab turned the corner and accelerated away.

"That was slick," Zach said.

"That's the basic evasion service. The premium level is more effective."

"What do I get for premium?" He didn't want to ask how much.

"Those two in the car? They disappear forever."

Whether Plenty was joking or not, Zach couldn't tell. They passed a dozen city blocks before entering a basement, a hangar of a joint populated with yellow cabs.

"You get out here," Plenty said. "I'll keep going. Take that door at the back. Wait in the lobby for five minutes, in case they have a backup car. Then catch another cab to your preferred destination."

They shook hands, and Plenty's cab took him away.

Probably had his new shirt picked out already.

CHAPTER 11

Donnie looked over the crowd and then back to his body. "It's weird for sure, but I don't feel dead." He inspected Keera more carefully. "You've changed. The way you look, lighter."

"I'm on your plane for now," she said. "You're seeing an essence of me, not the physical construct."

"Whatever. I feel the same. I feel fine."

"That's because it's your body that caused most of your pain, and now you don't have one." It was time to put a new thought in his head. "Your life here is over. You need to move on."

"I'm not going anywhere without my ring."

She tried another tack. "Tell me about the ring."

"Mez gave it to me."

"Was she your wife?"

"Should have been. She was beautiful in body and mind. Lived healthy, ate right, did all the things I couldn't do."

"Is that why you parted?"

Donnie didn't answer.

"Why is the ring still important?"

The ambulance doors were open now, and paramedics unfolded a gurney. Donnie said, "She told me that as long as I wore it, we would never really be apart."

Donnie and Mez were as apart as they would ever be, but he didn't see it yet.

"You wish you hadn't split up. Is that it?"

"Wasn't my idea, that's for sure." His face set, Donnie stared at nothing.

"Did she find someone else?" She deliberately targeted a sensitive area to get him to open up. It worked.

"No, she didn't." Donnie firm on this. "She said the drink and the weed had changed me too much. I wasn't the man she wanted anymore. I didn't believe her. Shit, even she liked what I liked, but she could stop. I never saw the point of that."

"When did she give you the ring?"

"That's the thing, you see. It was only six months earlier. An amazing moment for me, so when she started needling me to change later on, I thought she wasn't serious. If I was perfect then, I had to be the same guy now. Right?"

Wrong. Donnie's view of himself was colored by the intake of his favorite chemicals. He couldn't grasp how his behavior changed the mood of those around him. Mez must have given up and cut him loose.

He would figure this out, once he stopped fretting about the ring. This fixation, Keera understood—it was his only remaining link to happier times.

Some of the onlookers were leaving. One brushed past Donnie and shivered at the contact.

Keera said, "You notice what happened? That guy passed through your body like you weren't there. A smart person might figure he's dead after seeing something like that."

Donnie didn't agree. "I felt nothing. Saw nothing."

There was no convincing this guy. He wasn't going to shift his attitude whatever logic she threw at him. Time for a demonstration.

"Let's find the ring, shall we?"

Donnie brightened. "How we gonna do that?"

"You picture the ring in your mind and ask to be taken to it."

"Ask who?"

"Nobody in particular. Just ask." She wasn't going to waste time explaining to Donnie about his spirit guide. She could be jerked back to her body anytime if Zach arrived home noisily.

"You're not making sense."

"If you want to see that damn ring, then do what I say." She was close to shouting at him.

He closed his eyes and concentrated—and vanished. Faster than Keera had expected.

"Take me to Donnie," she asked quickly and hoped that Bardo was on the same page.

He wasn't.

Keera found herself in a restaurant. Zach at a table with an older, unkempt man. Volkov, presumably. Zach owned the only non-Slavic face in the room; the menu board displayed photographs of Russian food plates.

What am I doing here? She asked Bardo.

The usual: watching and learning.

I know how Zach eats; we share breakfast most mornings.

This is not about food habits. See what else you pick up.

What about Donnie?

He'll need your advice soon.

But I should stay here for now.

Correct.

Keera turned her attention to Zach, who was probing for insights in his usual casual, semi-joking manner. Yolkov wasn't giving much away, except when Zach stumbled into sensitive areas.

That the Russian was nervous about Zach's intentions was also apparent. She drew the only conclusion possible: Yolkov knew Rudin better than he wanted to. He held plenty of information—if Zach could extract it before more empty bottles piled up on the table.

The Russian was a drinker, and Zach wasn't even trying to keep up. Good boy. She watched as the waitress served food, maintaining a safe distance from Yolkov's hands. No need to be psychic to see their history: him groping and her pulling away. What a pitiful informant. Maybe it was normal; you take your information where you find it. But still...

The lunch drew to a close, Zach giving up temporarily, Yolkov warning him to avoid Rudin. As if Zach would listen.

What's Donnie doing now? She asked Bardo, anxious and wondering if she should have asked earlier.

He's quite bewildered. Who knew this would happen?

I thought you knew everything

Some things are hidden from me. I am not a god.

A god? Isn't there only one God?

There are many advanced entities, billions of years more evolved than you or me, that you would consider a god. But a Supreme Being? Your current level of development is insufficient for you to comprehend the nature of the universe. Shall we visit Donnie?

Is he still searching for that damn ring?

Worse than that—he's found it.

Bardo took her to a sparsely furnished apartment. Donnie stood beside her, staring at a woman slumped back on a couch. Donnie was on the spirit side, but the apartment and the woman were not. The way he remained transfixed by the sight of the woman told Keera it had to be Mez. But it wasn't just her physical presence alone that held Donnie's attention.

A silver ring lay in her palm.

Donnie became aware of Keera instantly. "How did you do this? I just thought of somewhere, and I ended up here? How is this possible?"

"When you're dead," Keera replied, "a lot of things are possible."

He kept glancing between Keera andMez. "Yeah well, whatever. Best weed ever, that's what I think." He pointed to the ring in Mez's palm. "This is doing my head in. How did she get it? She's not talking to me."

A man entered the living room, and Mez turned to look at him.

"Leggett, you sure Donnie didn't hesitate?" she asked. "Handed the ring over right away?"

Leggett was as skinny as Mez and twitchy as a canary. "Not for a second. I held out fifty bucks, and the damn thing was off his finger instantly."

Donnie lunged at the man, shouting, "You killed me; you took it." He threw a right hook that passed clean through Leggett's head. Undismayed, Donnie threw a left hook. Same result.

Keera said, "You can't affect anything in this room, definitely not people. That's because you're dead, see?" Donnie palpitated steamily beside Leggett but stayed in place. "I know how you feel," she added. "I'd like to whack him myself."

Mez said, "I can't believe how much he'd changed. When I walked past him last week I got such a shock. We split because he smoked too much but he always looked good, you know. But in five years…"

"I replaced her with whiskey, kept up the weed," Donnie said.

"Still had the ring, though, hadn't sold it for booze. Lucky for us." Leggett lit a cigarette. "Could be worth two hundred, three maybe."

"You bastard," Donnie shouted.

Mez looked up as if she had heard Donnie. "I don't know. The ring means something to me, more than a few bucks. I never thought when I told you about seeing Donnie lying there, you'd go back and buy it off him."

"You tell him, Mez," Donnie said. "Who is this creep, anyway?"

Mez looked over at Donnie, squinted. She's got the gift, Keera realized. She can see us—if she tries.

"Man." Leggett sucked hard on his cigarette. "I didn't go all that way for nothing. You told me about the ring, made it sound like it was wasted on him."

"That's not true; I was amazed he still had it. He must have needed the money lots of times, but he never sold it."

"It's you and me now," Leggett said. "Forget the past. Could have a real cool time with a few hundred."

Mez turned the ring around to show Leggett the inscription. *Donnie and Mez 1996.*

"If you want," he said, "I can have that removed. Be worth

more."

"You can't remove a meaning. It's not right. When I gave him the ring, and he saw the inscription, you know something? He cried. We have to return it."

"She's right," Donnie said. "I got real teared up. Happiest moment of my life, and I didn't know it."

Leggett dragged on his cigarette like it delivered emergency oxygen. "He needs the money."

"He can keep the money. I'll give him more, but I don't want a conversation. It took me forever to get over him."

"I ain't taking it back."

Mez glanced over at Donnie again, and her face froze.

"She sees you, but faintly." Keera jerked her chin at Donnie. "Move to her left; she'll see you better in her peripheral vision."

Donnie glided to Mez's side like someone approaching an old but estranged friend—slow and cautious. She remained still, face to the front, eyes fixed to the left.

"Donnie's here," she said. "I see him, not a quick flash of something that reminds me of him, but him. Actually, him."

"Hell you talking about?" Leggett said, crushing his cigarette in an ashtray.

"He's in this room." Her eyes widened in comprehension. "I can see his shape, more than that; he's smiling at me."

"You been sampling stuff before I got here, or what? You're not making sense."

"It doesn't make sense, but I see him. Not like I see you, but absolutely I see him."

"Maybe you're getting psycho, you know?" Leggett drew a fresh cigarette out of its packet. "The ring brought back a bunch of memories, and you kinda got worked up inside. Now you're seeing things."

"It's not psycho, it's psychic, and I'm not one. I don't know what's going on." She turned her head slowly to the left. "He's gone."

"She's lost sight of you," Keera said, "At her level she can't see if she focuses directly. She has some ability but no training."

"So, what do we do now?" Donnie asked.

"Nothing. My job is to guide you on your way. I can't, resolve leftover issues from your old life."

"Thanks for nothing. Well, I got news for you, lady. I'm staying with Mez until she dumps this piece of work."

Donnie's rescue was growing harder. But at least he'd accepted he was dead. Maybe.

"What do you think you can do?" she asked. "You can't affect anything physically. The most you can manage, and it's the worst thing, is to freak Mez out with occasional sightings of you."

"If she can see me, I can communicate."

"If she cooperates. She's more likely to think she's going crazy. Is that what you want?"

Mez said, "You know what this means?"

"Yeah." Leggett blew smoke. "We need to find you a cheap shrink."

"See what I mean?" Keera glared at Donnie. He didn't respond.

"It means Donnie's dead," Mez said. She swung around to Leggett, her horror growing. "How was he when you left him?"

"Sleeping like a baby, snoring louder than a busted exhaust pipe."

"I thought you said he was cheerful before, even waved you goodbye." Her face tight.

"Yeah, that too. Fell asleep right away, though."

Mez's eyes swept the room. She snatched up her handbag and pulled out aher phone.

"Who you calling?" Leggett asked.

"The cops, to see if they found a body in that area."

"Hey." He put a hand on her cell. "You can't do that. What if I was the last guy to see him alive? They'd suspect me."

"Suspect you of what?"

"I mean, if he's dead, he might have been killed, you know?"

"Killed? Killed?" She stabbed at the cell buttons, but Leggett ripped the phone away.

"What do we do now?" Donnie said in anguish. "We can't just stand here and watch."

"Let's see how this unfolds," Keera said feeling his pain while fighting her own emotions.

Mez scanned Leggett's face like she was searching for proof of something. They locked eyes.

Mez stood. Then fled.

CHAPTER 12

CHAPTER 12

Leggett gaped in disbelief as Mez threw open the apartment door bolts and vanished into the hallway. He ran after her.

"We gotta do something!" Donnie screamed. "He'll hurt her."

"We can't do a thing," Keera said and, not for the first time in her psychic life, wished it were otherwise.

"C'mon, I'm dead, right? I believe you, okay? You must be a guide or an angel or something. So, for Chrissakes, do something."

"I'm nothing like that. I have no physical power on this plane." She couldn't explain the pain that this lack often brought her: the pain of witnessing the living suffer no way to help.

"We'd better follow," she said, and they drifted behind Mez as she clattered madly down the stairs to the ground floor. Leggett lagged behind as Mez burst through the front doors, slamming them against the walls.

She ran fast along the sidewalk, throwing a look back at the pursuing Leggett as she darted out onto the road. The car she never saw hit her with enough force to hurl her over its hood, roof, and trunk.

"Mez!" Donnie flew to her side. Keera right behind him, almost paralyzed by shock. She hadn't expected this. All she had intended was to prove to Donnie that he was dead, and for him to leave. Now another person was dead.

Leggett pulled up panting; the driver vaulted out of his car to view the silent mess of a woman who had darted in front of his vehicle, and now lay behind it.

"Where did she come from?" the driver cried to nobody in particular. People gathered around, several spoke urgently on their cells, calling for an ambulance, the police, or a miracle.

Leggett knelt beside Mez's body and clutched her hand. Gently uncurled her fingers and removed the ring.

"Hey," the driver snapped. "The hell you doin'?"

"This is my girlfriend," Leggett said, putting the ring in his pocket. An ambulance siren yelped in the distance.

"You touch nothing until the cops get here."

Leggett rose to his feet. "You just killed my girlfriend," he said hoarsely. "You keep talking, and the next thing I touch will be your face with my fist."

The driver didn't back away. "You robbin' the dead? What kind of scum are you?"

"It ain't robbing. It's keeping our ring safe. You know cops, they'll steal it."

The yip-yip of new sirens announced the police. Keera wondered if Leggett was stupid enough to keep the ring after drawing attention to it.

She caught a movement near the body. Mez, a faint sketch of her former self, rose out of her body and floated to a watching position a few yards away, wispy as a trainee angel. Donnie approached her hesitantly. He too, had changed. The beard was missing, the clothes cleaner, and from an earlier decade. His face, his carriage, ten years younger. Mez saw him and smiled. Half in astonishment, half in confusion, all of it in pleasure.

They floated opposite one another, eyes for no one else, taking each other in, grasping their new situation. Around them, people milled, crowding around the body, oblivious to the lovers' reunion in their midst. Donnie held out a hand, and Mez took it. Even in spirit, her face glowed with joy as they came together and disappeared. They wouldn't be back. Keera knew it. Donnie and Mez had found each other again, this time for good.

He was the only one in her life. Bardo was back again. *She never settled with anyone else; she always regretted the breakup.*

Keera now understood why he'd asked her to take a left turn earlier. It was time for Donnie and Mez to be reunited and for her to facilitate the event. A whole new thought rocked her: bringing Donnie into Mez's presence had triggered her flight and subsequent death. Bardo would have known this.

"Are you saying I indirectly caused Mez's death?" Keera asked, shocked. "Do you have any idea how uncomfortable I am with that?"

Mez's time was up. You helped make the transition easier. You thought you were helping Donnie; you were also helping her.

Bardo often remarked that few humans grasped the arc of their lives any more than two-year-olds grasped why they couldn't have chocolate all the time. It didn't make her feel any better; it just stopped her asking further questions.

The paramedics lifted Mez's body onto a gurney; police questioned Leggett. He showed them the ring; the driver stood closely by until the police waved him away.

Bardo had gone, and there was nothing left for her here. She visualized her body back home, and seconds later she opened her eyes in her room.

There was no doubt Donnie had been sent her way for a reason. Despite Bardo's placating words, more revelations would surface in time. And Zach didn't need to know any of this. Let him work the physical plane; that was difficult enough on its own. To get him involved in Donnie's dilemma and conclusion served no purpose. The logic of the afterlife would only bewilder him.

Keera picked up her parents' phone and called Crime Stoppers. A witness who was unwilling to be identified, she told the operator, had seen a man strike a homeless person that she knew as Donnie, and steal his ring. Donnie died from the blow. Later that same man chased his girlfriend down a street, and she was killed by a car. The woman's name was Mez; the man's name is Leggett. He still has the ring. Donnie and Mez were involved in a previous relationship. An inscription on the ring says so.

"Oh my," the operator said. "Your witness is amazing. How could she know all this?"

"She's special: you have no idea how special and her story will check out. Leggett is a murderous thief. You find that ring; you'll have the proof."

"Thank you for your call. I'll give you a code, and if you have more information, please use this code next time you call. You may be eligible for up to a thousand dollars cash reward."

"I don't need it. Just catch that guy."

"Thank you for calling."

◆ ◆ ◆

Keera heard a car slow at the gates and knew it was Zach. She them and waited until he emerged from a cab. They held each other like they'd been separated for several centuries, but she didn't take her eyes off the cabbie until he was outside the gates again.

"He's only a cabbie," Zach said.

"Everybody is more than they appear." She took him inside. "You're lucky to see only their physical selves."

Her relief to see him clambering out of the cab was tempered by the sense that something else had happened after he'd left Yolkov. Something he might not share unless she told him she'd been at the meet. The next few minutes would be tricky. He wouldn't like her admission.

Zach pulled his customary homecoming beer from the fridge and sat at the dining table. She sat opposite him, arms on the table. "So, how did it go today?"

"The meet went well. I got confirmation of what you saw: that Dmitri was involved in a drive-by shooting in Brooklyn some years ago. Also that he's now active in data theft. I'm sure there's more info available from Yolkov."

"I know there is."

"What? How?"

"I was there with you." She tensed, waiting for the reaction.

Zach slowly replaced his beer on the table. "You spied on me?"

"I watched out for you. I had your back."

"You spied on me?"

"It's not spying," she said, "when you want to protect someone you love." Damn, she sounded so emotional when she was trying to be logical.

"It's always spying. I have a right to privacy."

"Not when you're in danger, you don't."

"That's the same argument the government offers when it spies on the good people of America."

"It's not. I care about you. The government doesn't."

"He took a swallow of beer and considered that."

"It's not that I don't want to tell you everything," he said, making a visible effort to calm down. "But some information can be disturbing and irrelevant at the same time. Why can't you trust me to tell you what I think you need to know?"

Unbelievable. He was using her argument when she'd decided not to reveal the episode with Donnie. "I don't know what you think I need to know. I prefer to know everything."

"Jesus," he muttered and finished his beer. Grabbed another one.

"Yolkov," Keera said, "is very connected to the killing I saw before. His aura became agitated when you brought it up. He couldn't wait to change the subject."

"I figured that out for myself, but thanks for the corroboration."

"Also, an ass fumbler. The waitress hates him."

"Knew that as well."

She rose and switched the kettle on, spooned loose tea into her pot. She didn't speak again until she rejoined him at the table. Gave him a chance to cool.

"What else did you do today?" she asked.

"Weren't you watching over me?"

"Not after the restaurant. I had stuff to do." She realized she might have said too much, and waited for him to ask what kind of stuff. But he didn't; his day must have been eventful enough.

"It was a quiet day, as you correctly sensed," he said. "I was only chased into the *Post* by two goons, hired a snoop to check out Rudin, and then had to flee back here to safety, using a backup crew and decoy cars."

"Two thugs chased you?"

"Not for long. The security guard stopped them and let me inside."

"What else happened?"

"I talked to a surveillance guy, Royston Plenty, and hired him to find Rudin."

"And then?"

"Afterward, I needed help to get out of the building, and this guy organized a nifty getaway."

"Anything else happen I should know about?" Say no, please.

"I came here."

"Are you sure that's all of it?"

"I have related all the day's events in chronological order, officer."

"Why didn't you call me from work? I might have been able to assist."

"I can handle a few things on my own, you know. Spying on me, for God's sake."

She came around the table behind him, leaned over and wrapped her arms around his neck.

"You have your ways, and I have mine," she said. "I know how to protect myself, but I'm not sure you do. You're a guy who jumps into situations confident you'll figure them out on the way. It's worked for you before. I've seen it myself. It won't always work, which is why I worry."

"I can handle this."

"Zach. They want a million dollars a week out of you. Wake

up. You're good to keep them happy for three weeks and then what?"

"Um, I've spent a few grand already. The snoop wasn't cheap." He seemed embarrassed about this revelation.

"Of course he wasn't. Funny how prices rise when people know you're desperate. If we have to dip into the dirty money, at least we're using it against dirty people."

"Well, the first thing is to find out where Dmitri lives. It'll give us an edge if he thinks we're more than a couple of easy marks. We have to strike back."

"Isn't that dangerous? We're not exactly a battle-ready platoon."

"Less dangerous than waiting for him to do whatever he wants."

"How would we strike back?" She sensed a half-crazy idea bubbling in his head.

"Not sure, but we can show him we know where he lives. That'll make him uneasy."

"How? Are you going to leave your calling card in his letterbox?"

"Maybe."

She sat down again and asked, "Are you thinking of doing something you consider heroic and dashing, but is really half-assed and stupid?"

"Certainly not. Looks like you're having a bad day at the mind-reading stuff, Keera." He swallowed beer to keep from smirking at her, she knew, but he couldn't conceal his delight at catching her out.

"I've have an idea," he said, "but it has to wait until we find Rudin's address."

PARKER RIMES

"This idea, you'll share with me then, right? Before you do anything."

"We're a team, we fight as one."

He was getting too cheeky. "Are you mocking me?"

"No."

He reached for her hand. She didn't remove it, but she didn't respond to his touch either.

"We had a good day, Keera," he said, holding her hand lightly as if he expected it to slap his. "We're no longer reacting, but gathering our resources to remove this threat to our lives. Be happy about this."

It took a few seconds, but she relaxed and responded to his conciliatory gesture by gripping his hand. He had a point. The events of the past two days had left her jittery, more than she realized.

"You're right," she said. "I'm letting those guys work their evil and rattle me. We have the situation in hand, as you say."

"That's the spirit. Let's be confident and buoyant." Zach toyed with his bottle, now empty. He wasn't making any move to fetch another. "So, how was your day, otherwise?"

"I got called away to help a dead man move on."

Zach leaned back in exaggerated surprise. "You busy thing. You were in spookland all this time."

"Not all day; it wasn't complicated. He was fretting about his ex-girlfriend, that's all."

"You get that sorted?"

"Sure, same old story. Boy meets girl, loses girl, gets her back again."

"Aw. And they danced along the shining path to the white light?"

98

"Don't be flippant. You'll change your mind when it's your turn."

"Whatever." He pushed his bottle aside. "You done for the night then? Feeling pleased?"

"Pretty much."

"We're not going to bed unhappy, are we?"

She rotated her cup in its saucer. "Unhappy doesn't describe the way I normally feel in bed."

"How would you describe your bedtime experiences then?"

"More like frolicky, pulsating, and wonderfully exhausting."

Zach pushed aside his bottle. "I'd like to test you on that, see how accurate your descriptions are."

Keera stood. "They're not descriptions; they're promises."

CHAPTER 13

At breakfast, Keera announced to Zach she was going to the university.

"I have student meetings, important ones to help people make the right academic choices for the future. I can't let them down."

Zach responded with alarmed eyebrows. "And your future isn't more important?"

"The students have been waiting for these interviews for weeks. It's a very stressful period for them." And dealing with routine academic concerns reduced the stress in her own life. A chaotic physical environment made for chaotic psychic signals; Zach should know this.

"Do you have any idea how rough these guys play?"

"I can dodge them. The university has several entrances and exits."

"They only need to watch one building: the one where you belong. Yuri would've told them you're a faculty member of the Department of Anthropology, and they'll be waiting."

"If I sensed any problems, of course I wouldn't leave here, but nothing comes to mind, and I'll go crazy sitting here all day."

"Didn't you tell me once that psychics are rarely psychic about themselves?"

"Rarely does not mean always."

Zach blew an exaggerated sigh. "I know I can't persuade you to stay, but I'm going to sit here all day and wait. A day filled with dread as the minutes tick by and you don't walk through the gates again."

She left the room to collect her pack, returned and kissed his face several times. "Every hour I can, I'll call you."

"You better."

"Even though you wouldn't do the same."

"Ouch."

"And I'll be ever so pleased to see you again when I return."

"Take two cabs, each way," he said, trying not to be deflected. "Make sure the cab goes right to the door. Anybody hanging around, especially two big guys, don't stop. Call me at once."

She drew away and, fishing her cell out of her pack, tapped on the Uber app. "The cab can drop me near an L, and I'll get another cab from there. I see anybody waiting; I'll do as you say." She pointed to her sneakers. "If I have to run, I'm ready this time."

He walked her to the front door. "Once they spot you, they'll try to grab you. This time, they'll have a backup. After I escaped them so easily, they'll be twice as organized. They'll follow your cab out and follow the next one you take. To here. Please don't go."

She activated the gates to open. "Should I go," she asked Bardo. No response. "Thanks."

A black Uber car eased through the gates and drew up in front of the door.

"Don't go," Zach repeated.

She enveloped him in a hug. "I'll be back, don't worry."

The Uber driver, a young dude, examined her with forensic attention as she climbed in. Until he caught her icy return stare. He faced front and drove off.

When she spotted a group of cabs outside a hotel, she said, "I'll get out here, thanks."

"You've paid to 56th Street," he said, stopping and turning in his seat.

"Changed my mind."

"No problem. Everything okay? You'll leave me good feedback?"

"The best." She climbed out and approached the yellow cabs.

She directed the next driver o the Social Sciences building on East 59th Street, her pulse quickening with every mile. The trip wasn't as smooth as expected. Her inner tension created as much turmoil as being chased.

By the time the cab reached her destination, she could barely breathe. She scanned the street—no men in long coats. No large men either. One skinny student, army coat, beanie, talking on his cell twenty yards away.

She walked briskly to the front door of the building, glanced back as the glass doors swung closed. The student wasn't talking anymore. He was staring at her, between throwing glances up the street, as if expecting someone.

She'd been tagged.

They had hired extra people to watch out for her. There would be watchers everywhere. No time to worry about it but still time to escape. She hastened along the corridor, hoping nobody stopped her to talk. Her purposeful stride acted like a ship's bow wave: parting the people in front. Except for one. Emma, a talented but anxious student.

"Hi," Emma said. "I hate to bother you, but can we discuss our meeting for later on?"

A meeting about a meeting? "Emma, I have to leave because of a family emergency. All the meetings are canceled. Can you pass the word on? I'll call all of you personally as soon as I can."

She flew out the rear entrance, leaving a gaping Emma behind. Working her way along walkways, crossing the inner roads, twitchy as a wide-eyed cat, heading north, and the hoped-for safety of the 55th Street and Garfield station further along it. Staying on university grounds as much as possible, away from the main roads where she knew the Russians would cruise, trying to pick up her trail again.

She stopped to check the GPS on her cell and saw the quickest way to the station was a straight line, almost. Through Washington Park that hugged the western end of the university. It contained mostly grassy areas with few trees, and she would have little cover, but no car could chase her through it.

Keera veered west and jogged to conserve her energy in case she had to sprint later. Sticking close to the lagoon, which offered the most trees for concealment, she worked her way to the other side of the park, and emerged onto the main road. She stayed on the back streets, running along 57th until she figured she was close to the station. Now she took a right toward West Garfield Boulevard and stopped at the intersection, blowing like a marathon runner.

Two hundred yards of meager cover: no parked cars on the street, only spindly trees on the center strip. This station was the closest L operating at that hour, and the Russians would be sure

103

to watch it.

What now, Bardo, she asked, they're going to have watchers up ahead? Still no response.

She looked around for inspiration or escape. No cabs came into view. Something else did—a bus. The stop was across the divided road, and Keera bolted to it, dancing through the traffic like a frenzied squirrel.

The bus was almost empty as she swiped her transit card and found a seat near the front. As the bus lurched forward, she gazed anxiously ahead and saw what she didn't want to see. Two men, big men, leaning against a car, watching passengers coming in and out of the station. As she observed them, one put a cell to his ear, and moments later, swung around to stare up 55th Street, toward the university. Her arrival had been noted, and the word put out.

The bus halted right next to the station, and the men's attention switched to it. Keera froze. undecided.

She'd be easy to grab before she stepped inside the station, let alone boarded a train. Best to stay aboard the bus. A Red Line station lay ahead. Regarded as damned sketchy by her students but even muggers were preferable to these two. She sat as still as she could, wishing she had an invisible cloak.

One of the men lifted an arm in her direction. Oh God. They watched as the bus doors hissed shut and ran back to a car. She swiveled to the rear window as the men drove up to the bus and then passed it. What the hell? The car continued onto the next stop and came to a halt. One clear thought came to her. They were going to board the bus and force her off.

Keera ran to the front. "Stop the bus now," she said to the driver. "I have to get off."

"I can't," he replied, staring right ahead. "You wait until we reach an official stop."

"If you don't stop, I'll vomit all over your dashboard."

The bus squealed to a halt, the doors clanked open, and Keera hit the ground, running back to the station. She could make it before the Russians could start up, find a traffic gap for a U-turn, and reach her. She hoped.

The rattle of an approaching train gave her hope. She pushed through the entry barriers, her hand shaking so much she had to swipe her pass twice.

She risked a glance behind but saw no one chasing. They wouldn't give up; they had to be close. She scrambled up the escalator.

The train doors were still open when Keera made the platform. She leaped aboard. Close the doors, she begged. Close the damn doors.

An elderly female straggler swayed past her door, burdened by too many shopping bags. A man jumped off the escalator; his eyes fixed on Keera like a homing beacon. He brushed past the woman jolting her sideways.

Maybe this woman was sick of being pushed around all day; perhaps she wasn't the type to take a backward step. Whatever the reason, she turned and kicked the man in the back of his calf. He tripped and hit the ground, his hands out, flesh tearing off as the rough concrete flayed his skin. Keera watched transfixed, as he slowly regained his feet, and the doors closed in his face.

She worked through the possibilities. They couldn't intercept her at the next station; they'd lost too much time. They'd drive to the one after that. Drop off one man to catch the train, and search it, while the second man carried onto the third station as a backup.

Their plan came to her as solid as if scribbled on paper and thrust into her palm.

Minutes later the train slowed to a stop. She was first out of the door and found nobody waiting for her. So far, she'd been right.

The train pulled out, the platform empty. Just her and her heavy breathing filling the sound space, while she stabbed at her cell, trying to locate the app for the local timetable. Then she didn't need to. The lines quivered and shimmied with the load of an approaching train. Going in the opposite direction. The best one possible.

Keera savored her moment of triumph as she rode the train south.

Her cell trilled. Zach.

"You promised to call," he said, angry and disturbed.

"I couldn't. I was running up stairs and jumping on trains."

"Trains? You caught two cabs, right?"

"Yes, but they were waiting for me. I had to go to plan B."

"Jesus! What was your plan B?"

"I ran for it. It's all good now. Coming home." She could sense the anxiety in him dissipating, but within herself, a cold fury refused to scatter.

"I don't know what you have in mind, Zach," she said, "but after this morning, I'll shred their evil minds until they're screaming for a padded cell and a bucketful of downers."

CHAPTER 14

Zach wondered how Keera, thought the laws of the jungle didn't apply to her. They had both discussed, both knew for sure, that Dmitri must have decided she was the key to the millions Zach could deliver. Yet, she'd waltzed off, figuring whatever happened, she'd master the situation.

The same thing she accused him of earlier. Good to know he was hanging out with a rational human being. Thank God she was returning home safe, maybe even a little smarter than when she left.

He called Edwina Moss, his City Editor. Time to explain his absence today, and for the near future. Hoped she understood.

"You're becoming a mythical figure these days, Zach," Edwina said. "People say they've seen you around, but these are only unconfirmed reports."

"I've stumbled across some New York Russians who are moving their base of operations to our fair city. Data thieves mostly, apart from any other ways they think of shaking money out of honest citizens."

"And you're undercover on this? Working on a story without clearing it with me first?"

Edwina still sounded pleasant enough, but she would change if the reason for his absence smelled phony. "The initial attempts at an interview didn't go well. The subjects proved hostile and left marks on my face."

"Oh dear. Your handsome face is now disfigured?"

"Temporarily. Time and good living heal all. Thing is, when I arrived at the *Post* yesterday, a couple of Russian heavies tried to intercept me. Only the presence of a security guard stopped them from taking me away."

"Lucky you."

He put her indifference down to her irritation at his absence. "I've talked to a Russian journalist from New York who's given me information on this guy Dmitri Rudin. Got another expert combing the data banks to supply more."

"My, you have been busy. To think I pictured you on a tropical island, escaping our crappy weather."

She wasn't listening, or his story sounded too dull to excite her. "Thing is, it's difficult for me to come in without being harassed, or worse. I'm hoping to work at home for now."

"And," Edwina drew out the word, "how soon will you appear and brief me?"

"I can brief you over the phone anytime."

"I like to see your face, whatever condition it's in, when you tell me what you're doing. You have two days, then we talk."

"But," he protested, "you know how long a proper investigation takes. Could be months."

"Two days." She closed the connection.

That went well.

He called Howard.

"I assume," Howard said, "by the lack of headlines screaming about a slain journalist that you arrived home safely yesterday."

"Sorry, I should have messaged you. Plenty was a very efficient getaway manager, and I thank you for introducing us."

"You're welcome. What sort of security have you arranged for your comings and goings in the future?"

"Ah, well, I was hoping to stay away until this story beds down," Zach said.

"A story? You have an actual story about these gentlemen shaking you down?"

"I figure a little limelight might scare them off." It was all he had. And the cash to buy information. And, if necessary, protection for himself and Keera. If she would accept it.

"And Edwina is comfortable with this?" Howard asked.

"She's not impressed, wants a meeting."

"Hardly surprising, dear boy. You have no evidence that makes sense."

"I thought my nose was sufficient proof I had touched a nerve somewhere."

"Oh, I thought it looked different, but I don't like to comment on people's appearances anymore. Fashions change so frequently I'm nervous about making a serious social error."

Howard was taking his usual discretion to a fresh high. "My nose was lacerated and bruised."

"True, but to me, it may have been a new form of self-expression among sophisticated types. Who knows?"

"I interviewed a crime boss. Hand gestures, theirs, are part of mob culture."

Howard laughed. "Perhaps you should adopt a gentler

method of interviewing. How did you find Plenty?"

"Smooth, charming, seemed professional. Disingenuous about his past."

"He's all that, with hardly any other faults to speak of. Anything you ask of him, he'll deliver."

Howard was saying nothing, throwing out empty words. Something was bothering him.

"But...?"

Howard paused before answering. "I don't know how much money you're involved with, Zach, and I don't want to know. But when Plenty sees money, especially a large heap of it, his attitude could change."

"Meaning what?"

"Be prepared, is all I'm saying."

"Howard, you're too dense. Spit it out."

"I've heard from others that Plenty's fee structure becomes highly fluid in these situations."

"Really? He wasn't cheap to start with."

"Of course not. He doesn't hanker to expose crime and corruption like you or me. He works only for the pay."

It was nice of Howard to warn him, but as far as Plenty was aware, the job was about finding data thieves for a story. Not much room for fee raising there. Newspapers had fixed rates for most contingencies, and Plenty would know it.

"Thanks for the warning," he said. "There's a growing complication. Keera. These Russians want to grab her and put pressure on me. She's not safe. They've tried to snatch her off the street twice."

"Really? Oh Lordy." Howard cleared his throat. "It sounds like you may need the help of the law. Is that a distasteful suggestion?"

"It would complicate matters, yes. The origins of this current situation are sub-legal, so to speak." The more he talked with Howard, the more he copied his manner of speaking. Made a note to stop this.

"So, the thought of a federal law enforcement agency coming to your rescue, hiding you and your beloved in a safe house, applying their vast resources to eliminate this threat to your lives, doing what your taxes are paying them to do, none of this would appeal to you?"

"No." That life could be so simple.

"Do you have a safe house at the moment?"

"Yes."

"Maybe you should get Plenty to sweep it, and install counter-surveillance measures?"

Howard's musings weren't helpful. If Plenty was interested in more money, he might, for a price, change sides. Letting him into their only safe place wasn't smart either.

"We're good," he assured him but the prickly thorn of doubt now nestled under his collar as he ended the conversation.

Sidirov called him ten minutes later. "My colleagues are disturbed; your first payment didn't arrive."

No preamble, no pleasantries. Such a pleasure to know people like this.

"Are they?" Zach said. "Are they as disturbed as I am that my girlfriend is being chased through the streets of this town? Not to mention a slight unpleasantness intended upon my person."

"You've confused them with another organization."

"I doubt it."

"Nevertheless, a situation exists where they need to reach an understanding. A meeting would be appropriate."

"If it's like the previous one," Zach said, "I'll skip it."

"That's not an option. You owe money, and in this matter there are certain formalities and procedures. You would know this, being a man of the world."

"I owe money?" What new tomfoolery was this?

"Sure. You offered a sum, you haven't paid it, so you owe it."

Eastern European logic had clearly drifted from the teachings of Euclid and Socrates. "Do me a favor," he said. "When you have a spare minute, write down the name of the school you attended. I don't want to send any of my children there by mistake."

"Ha funny ha."

"You know something, my friend," Zach said. "I'm rethinking the whole relationship. It's not turned out to be such a delightfully brief association as I had hoped."

"They'll be the judge of the term length. You just keep up your end of the agreement."

"I don't recall any agreement, but I do recall people asking for the impossible."

"Asking for the impossible," Sidirov said, "is the hallmark of a successful men. I'll report back regarding this conversation. Are you saying no agreement exists?"

"Pretty much."

"But you initiated the meeting."

"It turned out less than convivial. Nor did it fit in with my plans. Pretend I never called you. The money can find another home."

"That's not an option. My colleagues will meet with you again whether you want to or not. Your girlfriend will also be on hand, so there are no misunderstandings. They'll present their point of view frankly, and the atmosphere may become heated. But at the end of the meeting, you'll see how reasonable their position is. A rational man like yourself will have no problem arriving at the correct outcome."

"Which is?"

"You have to pay the amount expected. There is no alternative."

This was as bleak a future Sidirov could paint while talking over an unsecured phone. The Russians wouldn't give up; they'd grab Keera sooner or later and use her to force him to their will. Forever.

"There is another thing," Sidirov said. "The way you've avoided my colleagues has annoyed them. They're busy people, trying to put an agreement into action, and you behave like a schoolboy with secret agent fantasies. This is harmful to your interests and pointless. They know where you live."

He meant the apartment, of course. "But I'm never there. They notice that?"

"Yes. Your girlfriend hasn't come home either."

"How strange. I must ask her what she does at night."

"She hides with you, trembling like a little flower."

"In your dreams." He killed the connection.

Wait. Sidirov sounded very sure about Keera being not at home. He called her. No answer. Her phone switched to voice mail and, as he listened to her cheery message, his anxiety sharpened, and he wished his heart was stone.

CHAPTER 15

Zach opened the door as Keera walked up the driveway. "The fuck you do that to me for?" He pulled her close, holding so tight it felt like he might crack a rib to make his point.

His unexpected anguish engulfed them both, leaving her struggling to understand. He'd been calm and reassured when she'd called him earlier. Now he was a shipwreck.

"What did I do?" she asked.

"I talked to Sidirov after we spoke, and he said you'd be at the next meeting. I called to make sure you were safe, and you didn't answer."

He released her, ran fingers through his hair. "You didn't answer. Jesus."

She plunged a hand into her pack and found the cell under folders, stationery, tissues, and her wallet. The missed call indicator was on. "Sorry, I missed it."

He didn't react, face rigid.

"I thought I'd be fine to get home, forgot about calling you."

"All the time," he said, "I saw a van tailing you, snatching you

114

off the street. Later, your picture would pop up on my phone—sent by them." An unexpected skip in his voice.

"I'm sorry," she repeated, knowing words weren't enough. "Never happen again." She held him, not letting go, his silence screaming all his hurt.

"Standing here," she said, after a while, "in the doorway. We're exposed, aren't we?"

Inside, they sat at the dining table and Keera, not bothering to remove her coat, took his hands in hers. "I was stupid. Did the same thing I call you out for, forgetting there's two of us."

"Tell me," Zach said. "Tell me everything. Leave nothing out."

She left nothing out. The student watching, the two men at the station, the bag lady, the train switch, two cabs home.

"A miracle escape," he said when she'd finished, "and it won't happen twice. No help from Bardo?"

"None asked, none offered. That's the way it usually works."

He didn't respond, but she knew what he was thinking: what's the point of a guide who doesn't help you at bad times?

"I didn't want to ask. If he didn't reply, I'd know I had what I needed to escape—or that my time was up."

Of course she'd asked for help; it wasn't given. But frightening Zach with the truth would solve nothing. For all his skepticism, he'd have to feel more alone if he knew Bardo wasn't going to wave a magic wand and fix everything.

Zach had no further questions, no other bitter declamations. Once she'd made it clear she knew she had made a major mistake, and was sorry for it, his grievance lost momentum.

"It can't happen again," he said, the tension seeping out of him, his aura brightening. "That's the main thing."

"Damn right. I'm going to locate this Dmitri, observe him in his natural habitat, and show him who the hell he's dealing with. The Russians can be defeated with planning and intelligence. We only need time. And information."

"Plenty can find him," Zach said.

"Not like me, and not as fast."

If Bardo helped.

◆ ◆ ◆

"Do you know how many extra watchers I hired for the day?" Rudin asked coldly when Lev and Konstantin returned from the University.

"There was no point answering, as Yuri knew." Rudin would shout over the answer. Lev knew this, too. He made a pained face as if the wasted money came straight out of his savings.

"You," Rudin pointed at him. "You got the closest. You had her in your clammy fingers, and you let her slip away."

"She was lucky," Lev said. "The kid at her faculty said she figured him out right away, and must have run out the back. Otherwise, we could have surrounded the building and picked her up on her way home."

"The bus. You said you saw her on the bus, and you let her sit there. Did she wave bye-bye as she went past?"

"I didn't see. We were trying to drive to the next stop, jump on and drag her off. Again, she figured it out. How the hell she do this? By the time we caught up with her, she was boarding the train. This stupid old woman, kicked me, like she was in on it, and look." He showed Rudin his torn up palms."

"Ugh," Rudin said. "Put them away."

Lev walked into the kitchen and they heard him turn on a tap.

"Maybe," Yuri said, "they're listening to us. That girl Grigor saw must have planted a device."

Rudin said, "I was married a long time—nothing surprises me—but she's an enigma. It won't hurt to sweep this place. I'll get someone to come over."

About time, Yuri thought. A good general takes every precaution against defeat.

"This operation is costing me too much," Rudin said. "The whole thing was simple. Take the money off the reporter, find out how he got it, and then make him give us more. Forever."

"We roughed him up," Yuri said. "He doesn't like that. He's a normal middle-class guy, not used to those sort of conversations."

"He was a smart-ass."

"We threatened his girl. He hates that even more."

"How long have you been a confidant of his that you know so much?"

"I watched him for a night and a day. He cares about her more than anything."

"So," Rudin said, spreading his hands. "We know where to apply the pressure. We stop beating him, we start beating her."

"After today," Yuri said, "he'll move her to a safe place."

"He'd have done that already," Rudin said. "After the first time these two failed to collect her." He refilled his vodka glass and swallowed the contents. "Do any of you know how much this is now costing? I have had to hire extra people from local sources who, I should tell you, are not close friends and who are asking top dollar."

"We could contact the reporter with a fake story and grab him when he comes for the interview."

Rudin nodded. "It's an idea, but I've now put my Moscow boys onto the task; to find both of them. They're cheaper than local watchers, and computers never sleep."

"This could take months. What happened to the phone bug you mentioned?"

"It's coming. Software like this isn't cheap. The coder is asking seven figures. Negotiations are taking place. I expect a deal today."

He said it like it was up to him alone. Maybe it was. Many people, when faced with Rudin's negotiating style, suddenly saw his first offer in a more attractive light.

"And I'll add more people at the *Post* entrances," Rudin said. "Mr. Reporter will come for his car. Americans love their cars."

"We'll follow it? What if he dodges us?"

Rudin snorted. "We'll still be listening. He'll tell us everything we need to know. Today or tomorrow."

Later that night, Keera lay awake, alongside Zach.

I could have used some help today, you know, she said to Bardo.

Sometimes it's best if you endure the consequences of your hasty actions.

I tried to see ahead, but you showed me nothing.

And your conclusion was?

That I'd be fine.

The correct conclusion was to assume the worst and stay alert.

I spotted that student watching me, didn't I?

Thank God; you give me such nail-biting moments at times.

I have to locate this Dmitri Rudin, she said to Bardo. To find out how to block him acting against us. Can you take me to him?

The man can wait. There's another person of interest you should be aware of.

Zach wouldn't wake until morning; he was blessed with the ability to grab his eight hours sleep pretty much every night. She slid away from him so they were no longer touching. Any accidental contact with her physical body could bring her back before she was ready.

Bardo was waiting for her when she separated. "Follow me," he said, and his image faded to a small light which quickly drew away. She locked onto his light and found herself in a small apartment.

A man and a woman sat at a table, sharing a vodka bottle. Plates of pickles, cheese, and pickled onions lay between them. At first, their similarity made Keera think they were related, but she soon realized it was only that they were both Russians. They spoke in Russian, but she understood it at the unconscious level. She also recognized the man. Yolkov.

"The guy knows nothing much, Olga," he said. "But if he's any good, he'll turn up stuff that's not in our interests."

She had been right about him concealing stuff from Zach at the restaurant. Right about him being decidedly nervous about how much Zach knew.

"What's not in our interests?" Olga said. "If he can prove that demon killed my father, that can only be good."

Olga was much younger, in her twenties. Tall, blonde with an ill-concealed air of hostility. Keera was still unable to see a familial link between the two of them, but some bond existed.

Yolkov threw down a shot of vodka and slapped the glass back on the table. "There's a long time between making a credible accusation, and the arrest and trial. Rudin will have the freedom to move against people who can testify. And once Rudin's arrested, I can't get at him, but he can still send his men after us. Eliminate potential witnesses, in your case, and me for being involved."

"But Rudin doesn't know that you knew my father."

"He will if this reporter mentions my name in connection with that killing. He'll send his hackers to find out everything about me, including my whereabouts and, if I'm lucky, my choice of funeral arrangements."

Olga fisted her shot down. "So, if this guy locates Rudin, you get address, and we move fast as we can."

"He'll be surrounded by his security. What we need is a favorite restaurant. Somewhere open like that, where a single person can walk up to him and finish him off."

Yolkov didn't mean a word of it. Even an ordinary human could see that.

"As discussed," Olga said, "that'll be me. I'll press cold steel against his temple, and blast his brains across room."

God, she was a wild one. The worst kind, the kind that cared nothing for their own lives.

He scowled. "I promised your father, when I became godfather to you, that I would keep you from harm. You cannot do this. His men will drill you with more holes than you can count, faster than you can count them." He swallowed another shot at the thought of it. "Your mother, she'll die of grief."

Olga threw another one down as well. "She's not here, is she? Back with the family in Moscow. She'll understand. The avenging of my father's death is more important than a comfortable life." She tipped more liquid into her glass. "He was everything to me. Do you know what it's like to lose a father when you're only twelve years old? I adored him. A mother can never replace that bond."

"My father? I lost him to drink before I could talk. Be grateful for what you once had."

Yolkov settled into a brooding silence. Olga didn't look at him, popped a small onion into her mouth, and crunched down on it.

"When are you going to see this Bones again?" she asked.

"I hope never, but if he calls, I'll go. To put him off the scent if I can, to extract something useful if I can't. I have a feeling he'll bring more trouble than he's worth."

"Is that your old reporter's sixth sense working?"

"No, it's the fear-of-death sense that keeps me alive."

Bardo removed Keera. Not back to her body but her parents' home, to the living room, now filled with soft light. Seeing the familiar space from the next dimension was like peering through a fishbowl. The furniture soft and fluid, the colors muted. Bardo himself appeared almost solid.

"As you saw, the task of removing these people from your lives is complicated," he said.

"She really intends to kill Rudin?"

"Oh yes."

"Will she?"

Bardo raised his eyebrows. Wasn't saying. The future was not yet set, was what he wasn't saying.

"I get that Volkov's her godfather but how, if he was close to the murder victim Mikhail, how is it that Rudin doesn't know this?"

"Yolkov and Mikhail grew up together and were very close. They parted when Mikhail took his wife and the baby Olga to the

United States." He gestured with his arm. "You can see it here."

Space in front of her opened to reveal a scene of two men holding each other in an airport. The signs in English and Cyrillic. A woman and a young child stood by. She recognized the younger Yolkov; the girl could have been Olga.

A fresh scene showed the same two men, both older, greeting each other like long-lost brothers in an American airport. They talk; one of them, Mikhail she assumes, is excited. Yolkov is quiet. He's dismayed by what he hears.

Another scene and the two men are part of a family gathering, but there's a distance between them. The girl shadows her father, watching his face. She's in a party dress, and gifts cover a table. Yolkov smiles at her, but there's a sadness about him.

The scene faded, and she was back with Bardo.

"When Yolkov arrived a few years later," Bardo said, "Mikhail was already embroiled with Rudin. Yolkov wanted no part of it and stayed away. They met only on Olga's birthdays, which Rudin didn't attend. Rudin had no reason to know of Yolkov, let alone consider him a threat."

"I noticed he isn't so keen on retribution."

"Correct. He's out of his depth and hasn't the fire in the belly anymore. The alcohol drowned it long ago."

"So, where does that leave us?"

Bardo only smiled, shimmered into nothingness, and she found herself awake, back in her physical body. Zach exactly as she had left him. She'd give him the latest news in the morning. If she woke him now, he'd be up for the rest of the night, configuring every what-if and where-for until she was drained from thinking.

He didn't understand how his stresses, his highly charged brain activities, impacted on her. His vibes came through like a million darts at once, and she often struggled to subdue them so she could function.

Zach reached his conclusions through a conscious working out of whatever situation he found himself in. Often tempered with a flash of impatience and foolhardy impetuosity. His ability to bounce back from any setback gave him the idea that he could cope with anything, overcome any odds. A confidence that had cost him occasional and unnecessary punishments.

If he collected any more beatings, people would assume she had hooked up with a cage fighter.

They weren't far wrong.

CHAPTER 16

Later, Keera slipped out of bed to brew her morning tea. While she spooned leaves into the pot, she caught a movement in the corner of her eye. Donnie had joined her, standing by the doorway like a sheepish student.

"Do you need more help?" she asked him.

"No, life's good here. I thank you for what you done for me."

"Anytime."

"I feel I oughta repay you somehow."

Ah. Just what she needed. A confused, recently passed over, homeless guy to advise her from the other side.

"I see what you're thinking," Donnie said. "I don't know how, but I do. But I can help."

"Sorry. I didn't mean to think those thoughts. Listen. I'm fine; I have all the help I need, but thanks for the offer."

"There's bad guys looking for you."

"I know that."

"They wanna do bad things to you."

"Donnie? You're not cheering me up."

"I spent too much time getting loaded to develop those

interpersonal skills people talk about. But I'm trying."

"Thank you for trying," Keera said, "but I can manage. How's your life over there, anyway?"

"Kinda fun." Donnie brightened at the thought. "Sometimes, me and Mez hang out places we used to. Sometimes these places are like they used to be, and the next time they more modern. How's this possible?"

"It all depends on your attitude when you decide to visit there. If you're thinking of old times, you'll visit old times."

"I can change stuff just by thinking it so?"

"We all can. Even in physical life; it takes longer to change, that's all." It was too early in the morning for such deep philosophy. Keera switched on a kettle emphatically.

"I see you need alone time," Donnie said. "I'll be back when I can make a difference."

"I'd appreciate it."

He faded, leaving the air faintly cool in his wake. Keera stood for a moment, the kettle beginning to hum behind her. A ghost trying to be useful — there was something almost endearing about that. Almost. She poured the water, watching the leaves swirl and darken, and told herself that today, at least, she would keep things simple.

Zach woke up alone to the sound of kitchen clatter downstairs. Probably a sign he'd slept too long.

By the time he joined Keera, she'd prepared his morning coffee. Slices of toast sat in a silver rack. They were settling into a breakfast routine like a regular old couple. Or was she softening him up for bad news?

"Bet you were busy last night," he said.

She stirred almond milk into a bowl of oats. "I watched your Yolkov and his goddaughter discuss you, and their plan to kill Rudin."

"No. Please tell me you may be wrong. This could mess up everything."

"That's what I saw. I heard them discuss it. She's quite the firebrand; Yolkov was very uneasy about her plans."

How good was this? A reporter could sleep the night away while his personal, and beautiful, Jimmy Olsen roamed other worlds and brought back scoops.

"His goddaughter?"

"The man I saw murdered in Brooklyn was her father. Yolkov was a close friend of his. The daughter's name is Olga."

"Jesus, just what we needed. Somebody tries to whack Rudin, and I'll get the blame for it."

"He must have a roomful of enemies, Zach. A journalist won't be regarded as the first suspect."

He poured his coffee. "They have a solid plan?"

"They don't know where Rudin lives."

"Neither do we."

"Neither do we." Keera said nothing, and he guessed her unhelpful guide hadn't been forthcoming yet. "I'd have thought your first out-of-body stop would be Rudin. Didn't happen, eh?"

"I wasn't shown him, was taken to Yolkov." She sounded miffed.

"Well, I guess you can always go back and finish the job. We can't have sloppy detective work, psychic or not."

Keera ignored his ribbing. "What are you going to do today?"

"Talk to Yolkov, and reveal some of what we know, and see

how shook up it makes him. See if he can trade stuff."

"When?"

"Soon as I get my car back. I'll pick him up somewhere, and take him to neutral ground."

"Your car? Why risk taking it out of the *Post* garage? Rent one."

How to explain that a man needs his personal transportation when engaged on a tricky mission? A reliable and trusted vehicle. "It's a guy thing," he said. "I miss my car."

She gave him a resigned look but didn't press further. Which meant she didn't have bad vibes about the day ahead. He hoped.

When Keera returned upstairs to dress, he cleared the table and called the *Post* and asked to be transferred to Ernie, the security guard.

"Hi, it's Zach, the guy you helped get into work yesterday. I was wondering if you'd be out the back again today?"

"Same guys after you?"

"Same kind of guys, yes."

"Heh heh. You need a permanent security cordon, I reckon. I got front door duty until noon before I break for a half-hour. Tell ya something, I've already been out the back and seen a few new trucks out there. New to me, is what I'm saying. Those guys might have brought friends; you know what I mean?"

"Gotcha. I've another way in today." He didn't elaborate in case Rudin's goons had already approached Ernie.

"So, I don't have to practice my fast draw?"

"Not today, but thanks for the thought. Are you a drinking man?"

"Do I look like a teetotaler?"

"I'll send someone with a parcel for you. Enjoy in health."

"Some things I enjoy in any physical condition."

Zach killed the call as Keera reappeared. She didn't look like she was planning on hitting the town. Comfortable hiking pants and loose woolen sweater. Tight face.

"You okay?" he asked.

"Sure. I'll see if I can relax at home while you outrun the Wild Bunch."

He enfolded her in his arms, kissed her cheek, a couple of times. "It's not risky. They don't know when, or even if, I'm coming in."

"But how do you plan to get out? Yuri would have told them what you drive."

"I'll think of something, don't worry."

She snuggled closer. "That's so reassuring."

"You getting any bad vibes?"

"I'm trying to."

He laughed and released her. "See? Nothing bad will happen."

The first cab took Zach halfway to the *Post* before he made the driver stop at a liquor store. He paid off the cabbie and walked in.

"What's your best whisky?" he asked the skinny dude behind the counter.

The guy was calm, confident, and must have hidden an arsenal of weaponry under the counter to make him so.

"Is that whisky with or without an 'e'?"

The morning was too new for this kind of discussion. "Should I care?"

"Let me put it another way," the clerk said. "Domestic or foreign?"

"What's the difference?"

"It's not like comparing goat's milk to cow's milk. They taste different because of the ingredients, maturation and distillation techniques. It's important to be aware of this when choosing a blend for a special occasion."

Zach pictured handing a bottle of whisky to a security guard as a special occasion. "Best foreign."

"Scotch, Irish, or Japanese?"

"Sweet Jesus. Japanese, I think."

"Good choice, less peaty."

"Peaty?"

"Smoky flavor. Preferred in Scotches, but in some of them, the peatiness is rather unbalanced, in my view. I have a twelve-year-old Suntory. Would that suit you?"

"Leaving this store sometime today would suit me best. I'll take it."

Zach was still wincing at the one-hundred-forty dollar price tag when he left. The cost of security was rising. The clerk had thrown in a gift bag. Such a salesman.

Outside the store, he dialed up an Uber cab. Climbed into the back of a shiny black Honda SUV.

"When we get to the *Post*," he told the middle-aged woman driver, "can you drive into the carpark next to it? I'll give you my pass card to get in, and out again. I'm going to duck out of sight."

The black SUV wouldn't draw attention if it entered the underground carpark—it didn't look like a street cab. "Once you're back on the street, can you stop at the entrance, give it to a receptionist and ask her to send it up to the *Post* care of me? My name is Zach Bones. Here's an extra twenty for the hassle."

She turned south and swiveled around to look at him. "I've

never had that kind of request before, I have to say." She took the money and his card.

"You sure you work there?" she asked.

"Of course. I'm in a tricky situation right now. I want to avoid certain unsavory members of society, that's all."

"You been writing mean stuff about people?"

"Certainly not. A few individuals are trying to prevent the wheels of justice turning." His situation sounded pretty lofty when explained that way.

"It's a good thing some of the media still stand up for such things. Can't trust the government to act in our interests, can you?"

"That's right."

"Those politicians just lining their own pockets, right?"

"Whenever they can."

She fell silent then. Maybe she was organizing her thoughts for more pronouncements on the state of the country.

She wasn't. "These people. They won't damage the car, will they? It's mine, you know. We're all independent drivers."

"They'll be looking for a yellow cab; that's why I called you."

"So, you're not sure, then?"

"They want to talk, not stage a riot."

She reached over and flipped the glove box open, withdrew a shiny handgun, placed it on her lap.

"I'm armed, and licensed," she said. "And this is a new car."

Mother of God. "You flash a weapon and these men might get antsy and draw theirs. I just want to sneak in, not be in the middle of a gunfight. When we get close, I'll lie down on the floor and you drive in like you do it every day."

"I'll do what I agreed to do. But if these people get uppity, I'll draw on them. I don't go for this non-violent stuff; I don't have time for bourgeois niceties. This country was built with guns and pride; let's keep it that way."

He wanted to say that Rome was once built with swords and slaves, and then the Italians adjusted to modern times. But he held his tongue. The task was to slip past the goons, not debate the gun laws.

The *Post* building came into view. "I'm getting down," Zach said. "If any guys are standing out in front, don't stare at them. They're waiting for me, and they'll get ideas if you give them a chance to."

"Right. I go in the carpark, first on the left?"

"Yeah."

Crouched in the footwell, Zach waited as she slowed and turned left, paused at the boom, waved his passcard at the blue light, and slipped into the bowels of the garage

"When you see elevator doors at the rear, stop."

The car stopped. He climbed out.

"A man was coming over as I waited for the boom," she said.

"Did he see me?"

"He didn't get a chance. I took off before he got close enough."

The Russians were beefing up their watchdogs. Soon they'd be stopping cars and examining the interiors, while holding clipboards and pretending to be surveying garage usage or something.

He said, "Once you're out, can you give this to Ernie the door security guy? Tell him Zach Bones says thanks." He lifted the whisky, without an 'e', in its gift bag.

"All this for a twenty?"

Zach fished out another twenty.

"All this for forty bucks?" But she was grinning. "You're the most fun of the day. Call me direct next time; I'll give you twenty percent off." She handed him her card, waved him goodbye.

He caught the service elevator up to his floor. It opened into a hall near the office reception area. He peeked out. No goons. Nobody waiting. Nobody allowed to wait there. You were either ushered into the waiting room, or ushered out by security.

CHAPTER 17

Howard looked up when Zach passed him. "Have you seen this?" He indicated his monitor. "Maybe your boys are involved."

Zach checked the screen. A news site was breaking fresh news. "Massive Data Theft," the headline screamed. "City Hall Under Attack" blared the secondary banner. A quick scan revealed that the headline was reasonably accurate. Data records of several million citizens had been breached—private data,birth, death, and property tax records. No credit card numbers were compromised the officials said.

"My Russians?" Zach said. "Could be. But what's the point of having these records? I thought they'd go for credit card info and use it to buy stuff to sell for cash."

"Birth records are useful; fake passports fetch goodly sums on the black market. Edwina has given me this to chase up, which is why I'm asking you about those Russians. Seeing as how it's their kind of pastime."

"That Dmitri Rudin is in town if it helps."

Zach spotted Edwina weaving past desks, her eyes fixed on

his as she approached and halted in front of him.

"You know anything about this?" she asked, tilting her head at the screen.

"It's likely to be the same guys I'm chasing. Looks like a better story than I first thought."

She inspected his nose. "Oh my, you weren't kidding. You're supposed to ask easy questions, Zach, not try to beat the crap out of people bigger than you."

"My eagerness to please you made me overstep the bounds of good sense."

"I love a man with eagerness. What have you got for me? Glad you came in, by the way."

"I'm waiting for a guy to get back to me. A top-level security person, he's searching for the whereabouts of the leader of a data theft organization. All we know is he's in Chicago right now."

"You think he'll sit down for a searching interview?"

Edwina was moving to her sarcasm stage. Must be highly annoyed Zach hadn't gotten the data theft story first.

"I hope to interview a few ex-associates, the ones who aren't dead yet, and put a piece together. This might force the big guy to make a public statement, maybe talk to me personally. If nothing else, it will bring police pressure on him. This story can run for ages before any arrest."

Edwina considered for a few seconds. "Work with Howard on it." Patted his shoulder and walked away.

Howard said, "I was asked first, so technically that makes you my assistant."

"And I'm such an unruly one. You'll have to let me go my own way and dig up juicy tidbits for you to insert into the main story."

"That was my intention. But what do I tell Edwina?"

"That I'm organizing a second interview with a Russian, name of Peter Yolkov, who's familiar with Rudin's illegal activities in Boston. Has already linked him there to a fatal drive-by shooting."

"What went wrong during the first interview?"

"He became increasingly uncooperative with each bottle, and I terminated the lunch. I'm going back with fresh buttons to push that should free up his memory."

Howard said, "These fresh buttons, where do you find them?"

Howard wouldn't say it out loud, but he knew that Keera could supply more information, and faster than any dedicated researcher.

Zach said, "I have friends in strange places, always willing to help out."

"Good to hear." Howard swung lazily around to his monitor. "We should be able to crack the story wide open by the end of the week. Even win a major journalist prize later in the year. I'm so excited."

Zach called Plenty.

"Nothing solid yet," Plenty said when he answered his cell. "My best contacts are not available today. Big trouble at City Hall, you might have noticed."

"Funny that Rudin's in town at the same time."

"He's my first thought. It helps to check the obvious outfit's activity rather than search among the thousands who could have done this."

"While you're at it, can you locate the whereabouts of an Olga, who might be staying with Yolkov? Early twenties, no last name, a recent arrival in town."

"Will you have more requests this week? I'll engage more staff in that case."

And charge extra of course. "You're only searching for addresses."

"No chance that Rudin buys or even rents a place in his name. He'll use a corporate identity. I have to troll through corporate registers to find him or a name associated with him. This is what takes the time."

"Okay, I understand. Another thing. I need my car smuggled out of the park here. I think that you're the number-one guy I should turn to."

Plenty laughed. "A whole car is more difficult than a person, but it can be done. You at the *Post*?"

"Yeah."

"Stay there and wait for a call from a Diesel."

"Diesel?"

"It's a nickname. You'll find out why. He'll come in a small moving van. Put your vehicle inside it, yourself also if you wish, and he'll drop both items wherever you want. There'll be a mileage charge. I'll send you the invoice, fully itemized."

When Zach finished the call, he wasn't sure if it would be cheaper to pay off Rudin than have the money trickle out to Plenty every day.

He researched the latest Bitcoin price, created a virtual wallet which took forever, and with reluctant fingers purchased a million dollars' worth of Bitcoin. He left his holding there for safekeeping rather than move it to his laptop wallet. The loss of his password or irreversible damage to his hard drive would mean the instant destruction of the money. The benefits of progress. A million bucks sitting somewhere, but existing only as a sequence of numbers.

Late that afternoon, his desk phone rang — the *Post* reception. "Hi Zach, there's a man with a van trying to access the car park. A Mr. Diesel. He says you've asked for a personal delivery."

"It's true, let him in. I'm coming down to meet him."

"Your garage pass is here, too. You're not supposed to hand it out, you know."

"I must have dropped it in the cab I caught today. Thanks."

Diesel was leaning against his vehicle when Zach reached the parking level. Scruffy jeans, a beard from the Wild West, and cheery face that expected fun and games all the live long day. The van wasn't a van. It was a refrigerated compartment attached to a truck base. Nyugen Wholesale Meats it proclaimed on the side in fresh paint.

Diesel stuck out his hand and shook Zach's. "You got a broke down car, and you don't wanna let anyone know, 'cos it's embarrassing, right?"

"Something like that. You want me to drive onto this van?"

"You ever done it before? Steered up two skinny metal planks without falling off?"

"Er, no."

"Then let me be the one. Drive your ride up here and stop about ten yards back. You got a low rider?"

"No, it's a sixties Mustang. Plenty of clearance. Soft brakes, though."

"I'll allow for that."

When Zach pulled up behind the van, Diesel had already extended two metal ramps. He took over Zach's seat and reversed a few yards. Gave the thumbs-up signal, grinned wide as a letterbox slot, squeaked the tires, and roared up the ramp at light-speed before jamming the brakes on inside the van.

Diesel lowered the roof and climbed out over the seats. "Bet that made your heart race."

Race? My heart fucking stopped. "Nah, I heard you were cool."

"Where do you want your car delivered?"

"I'd like it, and me, taken somewhere isolated and left to drive away."

"If I unload you in a street it'll attract attention. How about a closed warehouse, about thirty minutes from here?"

"Sounds perfect."

"Hop in your car. "The compartment's airtight, but you'll be fine for an hour or so. After that, the CO_2 build-up starts to kick in."

"You serious?"

"It's okay, it takes hours to die. You'll be out of there in thirty minutes."

"Do they call you Diesel because you like speed, or because you drink the stuff? I'll ride up front, thanks."

Diesel said, "When I drove in, while I was waiting for the boom to open, some guy came up and looked inside the cabin. Looked real careful. You wanna take a chance they won't be waiting for me to come out?"

Zach walked up one of the ramps and vaulted into the Mustang's back seat.

"I'll turn the refrigeration unit on," Diesel said. "That way the van looks like a working meat van with a noisy fridge, not a box with a hidden cargo. I'll turn it off after we get out of the immediate area. Otherwise, you might catch a cold."

When the van door slammed shut behind him, Zach flinched.

He took calming breaths and tried to recall the patron saint of oxygen.

Thirty minutes later, he was queasy from the motion in a locked box, and a headache was kicking his skull apart. With the refrigeration off, he was hot, clammy, and anxious with increasing claustrophobia. He opened Google to check the symptoms of CO_2 poisoning, but the van stopped. The back doors opened, and he sucked in cold, fresh air like a surfacing whale.

"I know what you're thinking," Diesel said, as he rolled out the ramps. "The view in there ain't much, but it's a helluva experience, eh?"

Outside, Zach steadied himself against the van, pressed his forehead against the cool metal. "It's a helluva something, that's for sure."

CHAPTER 18

K eera lay on the sofa and closed her eyes. This time, she said to Bardo, please, I'm begging you, please take me to Dmitri Rudin.

As you wish. Bardo didn't manifest, connecting only as a voice in her head.

With Bardo's help, separating her consciousness from her body wass far smoother than when she tried by alone. Seconds later, she floated near the ceiling of a large room where two men sat on opposite couches.

She recognized them both—Rudin, older now, and Yuri.

Yuri Buteyko, who had once helped kidnap her, and who had later shot a co-kidnapper to save her from rape. Who should have been sitting in a cell somewhere in Phoenix awaiting trial for murder. What was he doing here?

"You still think," Rudin said, "these two are connected with some stupid secret organizatioHe spoke in Russian but she could understand all of it.

"I was convinced early," Yuri replied, "and nothing has changed my views. This organization is not stupid; they are invisible. Bones and his woman are protected. Not hundred percent, because we almost grabbed her, and Bones wasn't warned about meeting us either. But somebody is watching over them, and they've now hidden them. This is why Bones was so insolent to Sidirov yesterday."

"The prick. He needs reminding of his position." Rudin took a sugar lump from the bowl and clamped it between his teeth. He sipped on a tall glass cup of tea sitting in a gilded metal holder, the tea coursing over the sugar for sweetness. A plate of cakes lay in front of him. Sugar held no fears for him.

Yuri wasn't a tea man. A shot glass huddled next to a vodka bottle, but he wasn't throwing down shots. Maybe mornings came slower in his post-arrest world.

Keera scanned Rudin's aura; muddy browns and blacks that indicated high levels of negativity, an individual who trusted nothing or nobody. He saw the whole world as an enemy.

Am I right? She asked Bardo.

Yes, and he's not easily frightened, he regards himself as invincible.

Will he find us?

Stay alert.

What will stop him?

Nothing. Zach's offer unleashed new imaginings that are driving him to new expected outcomes.

Yuri said, "If Bones is in hiding, all we have is his cell number."

Rudin sipped tea. "That's all we need."

"So we call him daily, and exchange small talk, and he agrees to our proposal?"

"You're not as funny as you think. If I want a clown, I'll hire one with big red nose."

"I apologize. But how is this phone number so useful."

Rudin took a long sip, made Yuri wait. "There's software. We install it on any phone with text message or email. The guy doesn't even have to open it; the software installs in seconds and works right away. My boys can listen to conversations, take pictures with camera, download files and intercept Skype calls."

"*Mater Bozh'ye*, Mother of God," Yuri breathed "So now we know where he is?"

"Soon, soon. If he calls a cab to his address, we have him."

"What if he notices this software?"

"My boys tell me only sign is extra data usage. And who checks that unless they have a shit data plan?"

"Amazing." Yuri shook his head in wonder. "What if he shuts the phone off?"

"Doesn't matter, this little bug keeps working." Rudin leaned toward him. "We installed it an hour ago. Now we wait. Soon as he talks, we'll figure out where he is."

Keera hovered, paralyzed with shock and indecision. She had to warn Zach, but she might miss out on more vital information if she left. And Zach must have retrieved his car by now, and would be driving to Lake Forest. As long as he didn't disclose their address on the phone, they were still safe. She waited.

Yuri swallowed a vodka, brushed his lips with the back of a hand. "They'll be together; I saw this before, they don't like to be apart. Find him, we find her."

Yuri appeared pleased, but Keera saw otherwise. His aura

glowed a sudden, violent red, suppressed anger flooding through him.

Why is he angry?

He feels humiliated because he wasn't consulted about the bugging decision. His status is important.

"When they're together," Rudin laughed, "we'll hear them making love. My boys always enjoy those moments."

Bardo, Keera asked, do we have to kill him to be rid of him? She surprised herself with the question. The more she came into contact with the earth's lowlife, the more she drifted into the same brutal, callous patterns she observed. As if the worst evil exuded the strongest gravitational pull.

You will not succeed.

Yuri said, "You should have installed this earlier. We'd have them by now."

"No shit. Who knew Bones would get so high and mighty and dump the deal. After all, he contacted us."

"Should have bugged him right after he resisted."

"Sure. I snap fingers and new people appear to help. I am businessman, not a genie. Once the software is installed, I hire extra people to collect output. This takes time."

"Can we track the phone, like GPS?"

"*Nyet*. Promised in next upgrade."

Rudin's cell beeped. He answered it, listened, and his face grew relaxed and cheerful. "Good work," he said. "Tell boys I'm very happy." He closed the connection and tapped out a new number. He said to Yuri, "They are hearing Bones, and another guy."

A voice answered the call, and Rudin said, "We can hear Bones talking about a meat truck. This mean anything to you?" A pause. "They're talking about driving a Mustang up inside it, and going somewhere else to let him out."

The voice replied, fast and agitated. Rudin scowled. "Okay okay, keep watching." He killed the call.

"We nearly had him," he said to Yuri. "A meat truck drove into the *Post* carpark and left after ten minutes.'s was inside, and his car. We're looking for a red Mustang. With our clever little reporter driving."

Relief flooded over her for an instant until she grasped how close Zach had been to capture. She had to return to the physical and call him. The Russians would hear her call of course, but it had to be that way. She couldn't afford to wait until they were alone, and his phone in a bucket of water.

I have to leave, she said to Bardo.

Wait.

Yuri said, "How did he get inside the *Post* without us seeing him?"

"In anybody's automobile trunk, if he wanted to. But we'll find out when he talks to the girl."

"Let's get our communication lines working faster," Yuri said, his aura still pulsing red. "I can be the contact guy."

Rudin picked up his tea by the holder, touched the glass with two fingers, and put it down again. "Cold tea, an American habit I avoid. I am successful, Yuri, because I stay at center of the actions. All of them. A chain of command, or a chain of communication, often breaks down."

"We should've told the watchers sooner."

"They got data seconds after I did. Don't worry."

Rudin's cell beeped again.

He listened to the new caller, grunted approvingly, and

cut the connection.

"My boys also found a way into City Hall last night," he said. "We hold data on every household in Cook County. The news is all over media."

Yuri stared. "I didn't know we were targeting the County."

Rudin shrugged. "Why would you?"

Yuri's aura exploded into fiery arcs of red and orange.

Before leaving the Russians' house, Keera drifted outside. The exterior was pink stucco of no particular style—two stories, with low-maintenance gardens flanking a curving driveway. A tall hedge hid most of the house; a pair of pink metal gates guarded the drive.

Out front, a well-built man smoked, leaning against a BMW SUV. She fixed the image of the house in her mind and drifted to the street where she located the street sign and house number. As she sank to letterbox height, a yell burst from down the driveway.

"Hey, you!" the driveway man shouted, sprinting toward her.

What the hell? He sees me? She asked Bardo.

He's one of the few who can.

He was closing fast, ten yards away, only the gates, unlocked, between them. Torn between allowing him to run right through her image, and shocking him into stillness, or fleeing, she decided it was best to let him believe she was real.

Keera slipped sideways behind the hedge, and as the man reached the end of the driveway, she pushed through the hedge and settled behind the BMW. She watched through the BMW's windows, certain he couldn't see her through the glass and distance.

He didn't, but he didn't give up either. He disappeared through the gates and behind the hedge. She floated to the rooftop level to watch him running to each corner and checking the side street. He ran back up the driveway as she slid behind a chimney stack.

The man was thorough; he drew a gun and sprinted around the side of the house, and continued until he'd completed the circuit back to the front. His chest now heaving, his mind doubtless tormenting him with what he couldn't explain.

He entered the house and returned with Rudin and Yuri. "She was snooping by the gate," he said, pointing down the drive. "I ran to her, and she was gone. Checked the street corners, either side. No one. I scouted the perimeter: still no one."

"She drove off in a waiting car," Rudin said.

"I would have heard it."

"Not an electric one, Grigor."

Yuri asked, "What did she look like?"

"Black hair, and a dark sweater. Loose pants. Happened fast."

Yuri glanced sharply at Rudin. "Like a special operations unit."

Rudin said, "You stupid or what? Black is popular; most of my boys at home wear it. Think they're special forces or some shit."

"She fits the description of Keera Miles."

"So do a million shopgirls."

"Thanks for the compliment," Keera retorted, unheard.

Grigor waited for Rudin to issue orders. She picked up that the guard was still rattled about seeing her and losing her so fast. It couldn't have been the first time this had happened to him, but his manner suggested that somehow, this time, was different.

Maybe she'd been more visible than other apparitions he'd glimpsed. Maybe the earlier occasions had been more fleeting, and he'd dismissed them, but today he couldn't.

"Let's be extra careful," Yuri said like he was addressing his troops. "We're in a delicate position, and we have a snooper. It will repay us to exert the utmost vigilance."

Rudin turned to him. "The fuck you talking about? I'll explain whatever the fuck needs explaining. Got it?"

"I'm stating what we all agree on."

"Then why state it? Keep your tongue still until I ask you for an opinion."

Yuri's aura, which had calmed to a steady yellow-orange, sparked back to a flaming red.

Zach kept bursting into her thoughts. Please take me home, she asked Bardo.

She opened her eyes in the living room and struggled upright to find her phone. Jittery, and still buzzing from the last twenty minutes on the astral, she stumbled into the kitchen area. The phone lay on the table and she stabbed at the screen with unsteady fingers. Jammed it to her ear. Voicemail. Zach on a call. His phone was never switched off.

Shit.

She killed the connection. What to say that wouldn't give away every advantage they possessed? She briefly considered finding him astrally, but she was too shaken to get back there. It'd be quicker to text him.

Keera dictated her message. "Do not use your phone," she said, firmly as she could without shouting. "Don't even talk if the phone is in the same room. Call me immediately from another phone. It's freaking urgent."

She watched the words spill across the screen and, satisfied that her message had been translated accurately, pressed the send icon. All she could do now was wait.

Thank God they couldn't trace phones with their software —Rudin had confirmed it. But they *could* download files, he'd said. Did that include Zach's contacts? If so, her number was available for them to infect. But they hadn't done that yet; Rudin would have said so.

She'd tell Zach to bring home two new phones. And new SIMs. And maybe find out how to remove the bug. God. She stared at the phone. The screen came to life. No caller ID. Not Zach's phone.

"Hello?" she asked, knowing a dozen people could be listening.

"It's me," Zach said. "What's up?"

"Look, I think my phone mightn't be secure either. We can't talk." She sounded like an actor in the worst spy movie ever. To the listeners, it would only confirm their suspicions —that she belonged to a clandestine organization.

"You sure of this?"

"Hundred percent. Come home now. Whatever you do, don't identify anybody or any address on your phone."

"Oh shit."

CHAPTER 19

Zach shook off his brief attack of claustrophobia and suffocation by dropping the Mustang's top and flooring it down the first empty street he found.

The euphoria didn't last. Plenty called. He slowed and picked up his phone. "Yeah?"

"This Yolkov person?" Plenty said. "I have his details."

"Love your efficiency."

"He was easy to find, not trying to hide. I assume he's not one of nature's villains."

"He's a not-so-helpful pain in the butt, is what he is. Your information should make him more cooperative. Can you email me the details?"

"There's more," Plenty said. "A woman known as Olga Petrova gave the same address when she entered the country two days ago."

"How do you know?" Keera's information confirmed by Plenty, no less.

"I wouldn't pass on information if it weren't authentic, would I?" Plenty staying patient, but letting Zach know the

149

question was frivolous.

"Yeah, but that was quick."

"That's the business I'm in, the business you're paying for."

"Who is she?"

"Her visa says she graduated in mechanics and mathematics from Lomonosov Moscow State University. That's the alma mater of Mikhail Gorbachov, in case you're interested. She is also a top athlete and made the University Sports Shooting Team."

"She's here to take part in a shooting tournament?"

"Not that we know. "Her visit's stated purpose was to meet relatives, which isn't strictly true. Yolkov isn't one." I could, for a fee, ask Homeland Security to expel her for lying on a visa form. But they may not listen to me without evidence of planned wrong-doing."

This was good to know, but Zach had no evidence that could be shown to any Homeland guy. Gathering evidence while out-of-body was not yet recognized as reliable witnessing.

"I'll keep that in mind," he said. "Thanks for your help."

"I try to assist. I meant to ask: do you clean your phone with an anti-virus regularly?"

"Sure. Every month."

"Seriously? In your business?"

"I've had no issues yet. I can spot spam and phishing easily enough."

Plenty grew stern. "That's amateur stuff. The kind of guys you're up against have access to software you've never heard of."

Plenty was upselling him; Zach didn't even ask how much it would cost.

"I'm good for now. Will let you know if things change."

"It's your decision," Plenty said. "But after seeing the kind of people you are involved with, I'd be more particular about security. I can block all the latest listening devices."

"I hear you, but I'm not acting yet. Thanks again." The way Plenty saw extra profit in every corner made it likely that the final bill would stretch to five figures. It wasn't his money, but still.

Plenty cut off immediately, and his email with the address details arrived a few seconds later. Yolkov lived five minutes away.

The block of red-brick apartments had probably looked promising on a drawing board once. Now it just looked tired. It would be others who faced the grim reality of the finished product.

He called Yolkov.

"You again," he answered. "I'm not hungry today."

"I didn't get much for my money last time, so we have to do it again."

"You got all you can get."

"Not true. You're holding stuff back. Let's talk some more."

"Why don't you take a long walk in woods, and stick your head up a dead bear's butt?

"Such language in front of a lady."

"What lady?"

"That nice Olga staying with you," Zach said.

Yolkov sucked in air. Silence for a whole minute.

"The fuck's going on?" Yolkov said, regaining his bluff feistiness.

"I'm trying to remove Rudin from my life. I need your help. Come outside and get in my car."

"You outside?" Yolkov said, both amazed and angry.

"I know, I know, it's so impolite to drop by without calling, or even an invitation. But why don't we go somewhere enchanting and exchange confidences again? I'll buy the best vodka for you to take home."

Long pause.

"Give me five minutes," Yolkov muttered.

He came through the entrance looking the same bedraggled wreck as the last time. Maybe he hadn't had time to change. It'd only been two days.

He wrenched the passenger door open and thrust himself inside. He pointed a finger at Zach. "Don't ever mention Olga again. It's too dangerous. For you, for me, and especially for her."

"But she's part of the problem, isn't she?" Zach slipped the car into gear and pulled away from the curb.

"She does not exist," Yolkov shouted.

Zach turned north. "Let's find a quiet place. It's such a sunny day; I'm thinking Lincoln Park, a comfortable bench, trees, and birds. What do you think?"

"You promised me best vodka. I assumed food would go with it, but it's not deal-breaker." Yolkov wriggled in his seat and fastened the seatbelt with difficulty. Had probably started drinking already.

"You'll get your reward, but I need something in return."

"I told you all that's useful. I don't know where Rudin is staying."

"That's not my concern today; we'll find him soon anyway. I want to know Rudin's biggest weakness, or any of them."

"He hasn't got any."

"Everybody has one," Zach said. "Usually more than one."

"Mr. Reporter, he doesn't care about anyone or anything

except accumulation of money."

"Then that's his weakness."

"It's everybody's, isn't it? You have such a talent for the obvious."

Zach swung into Lincoln Park, heading away from the zoo. The smell of huddled, bored animals wasn't his favorite thing.

"The whole reason Rudin is interested in me," Zach said, "is he thinks I can access a lot of money."

"Can you?"

"Not as much as he wants."

Yolkov laughed. "Nobody can satisfy that guy. He could empty Fort Knox, and still ask, 'Where's rest?'" He caught Zach's eye. "It seems you need me more than I thought. You know squat about Rudin. No hard facts."

Zach stopped at an intersection. Drummed his fingers on the wheel. "You want facts? Here's some you'll enjoy: Olga Petrova is the daughter of Mikhail Petrov, the man Rudin shot dead about ten years ago. She arrived in the US of A two days ago for one reason—to kill Rudin. With the unbelievable luck that killers often enjoy, she found out through you, who found out through me, that Rudin was in the same town."

He shot a glance at Yolkov. The guy had his mouth half-open. "Here's another fact: you have little control over her, and if she sees a chance to blast Rudin, she will, no matter what the consequences are. Final fact: if we don't work together, and she goes with her Lone Ranger thing, she'll die. And you and me? We'll be so close to death we might as well lay out our burial suits now."

Zach stopped his car in the park with a view of a small lake. Peeked at his phone. He'd missed a call from Keera, but she'd left no message. He made a mental note to call her after he'd dropped Yolkov back home. She might get nervous, angry nervous, if he didn't contact her. Just like he had yesterday when she'd forgotten to stay in touch, and left him abject and fearful. Hey, sometimes, the karma bus arrives fast.

His phone pinged the arrival of a text message. Keera. He stared at her message in confusion at first, his jaw tightening, before switching the phone off. For most of the last hour, Rudin had listened to all his conversations. He climbed out of the car and placed the phone on a fence railing ten yards away. Picked it up and moved it another ten yards.

Returned to a fascinated Yolkov.

"Your phone?" he asked, putting out his hand. When Yolkov didn't move, he added, "Mine could be bugged. I have to confirm it. This concerns both of us."

Yolkov sat still.

"If you don't hand it over," Zach said, as evenly as he could manage, "I'll tear your clothes to rags until I find it. And when I've completed the call, I'll shove the phone so far down your fucking throat it'll poke out your ass and make your ride home very uncomfortable."

Yolkov tugged a small flip-phone out of a pocket. Zach closed the door, assuming his conversation would be shielded from his own phone by glass, metal, and distance. Also assuming Yolkov wasn't Rudin's man in secret. He called Keera's number and listened to her curt explanation, each word driving a spike in his chest. He should have listened to Plenty's advice. Today's karma bus was a double-decker.

Zach snapped the phone shut and handed it back. "I think we're about to descend into hell."

"Both of us, or only you?"

"Rudin was listening. He knows where you live, he knows Olga is with you, and knows she is coming to kill him." He pointed to Yolkov's phone. "Call her, tell her to get out *now*."

Yolkov sat immobile.

"Call her," Zach shouted. "I don't want her death on my conscience."

Yolkov opened the phone with palsied fingers and stabbed at the buttons. Somebody answered. Yolkov spoke Russian, his voice speeding up and rising until he was almost shrieking.

Olga, if it was her, was obviously dismissive of Yolkov's urgent suggestions. Another one of those who thought harm only came to others. After a minute of this heated exchange, Yolkov's attitude switched to relieved gratitude. Olga must have agreed to flee. He closed the call. Stared through the windscreen at a future only he could imagine.

"What about you?" Zach asked. "It's not safe for you to return either."

"They don't care about me. I'm old and shaky. If I had wanted to avenge Mikhail's killing, I would have done it years ago, but I was too scared."

"Whatever. But they'll use you to get at Olga. They tried that technique on me. You have to hide as well."

"Take me home. Forget vodka."

Zach retrieved his phone from the fence, and locked it in the trunk, under a blanket. Hoped that would kill it as a listening device. He opened the glove box and pulled out his previous phone. Dead battery, of course, but he plugged it into the car charger and drove them away.

"Where's Olga going?" Zach asked.

"None of your business."

"I don't want to sound heartless, but if you're gunned down in the next hour, I'll feel an obligation to her. I can shelter her."

Yolkov laughed without humor. "You just dumped her in front of firing squad, and you still pretend to be nice guy?"

"I didn't know, and I'm trying to fix it. What does she look like?"

"Like a beautiful young Russian with murder on her mind. White face, black heart."

The old guy was leaning on poetry to get him through the day. Probably quoting Pushkin. All Russians did.

"That's not very helpful if I have to find her in a crowd."

Yolkov didn't reply.

"If you don't care about your skin or her skin," Zach continued, "I'm still interested in keeping mine intact. We have to assume they'll be arriving at your door any moment. They'll grab you if they know what you look like, and they'll surely carry me away to say hello to Rudin."

"So?"

He sounded resigned to his fate.

"If you insist on returning, I'll drop you a couple of blocks away, and good luck for the rest of your life—the whole half day left of it. But for your conscience, you have to tell me where to find Olga."

Yolkov dug fingers into his jacket and withdrew a small revolver. Flipped the cylinder out. Fully loaded. Snapped it back. Kissed the barrel.

He said, "I won't die alone."

Jesus. A whole new Yolkov was sitting next to him—a crazy new version. "I didn't mean you should go down fighting," Zach said. "I'll take you to Olga, wherever she is. I'll help you find a safe place. Any hotel you want to name, I'll pay for it until Rudin's gone."

"No. An actor once told me, the way to get through life is to always to show up, even when you're scared. I was once too scared to avenge Mikhail. A stupid, cowardly mistake that brought me to this moment. I'm still scared, but now I have no choice. Whatever happens, happens."

"Sure you have a choice. Don't be such a drama queen."

Yolkov swiveled around to face him. "You don't get it. Rudin now knows Olga will kill him if she gets a chance. And he knows she's connected to me, so he'll know I'll come after him if she dies. He has to eliminate both of us. Nothing will stop him except his death."

The day had started so well with small triumphs and had promised so much more when Plenty supplied Yolkov's address. Now it was about to end in the worst way possible: a man dragged into Zach's problems, and unwittingly sentenced to death. His goddaughter as well. Nothing in journalism school had prepped him for this.

"For God's sake," Zach said. "Please tell me where she is, and we'll go there. To safety."

Yolkov didn't respond.

Zach tried for the low blow. "You owe Olga to stay alive." No response. He slowed the car, and it passed along the street like it was part of a funeral procession, without the sobbing.

A few minutes later, Yolkov said, "Stop here."

Every atom in Zach's body screamed at him to keep going. He stopped.

Yolkov climbed stiffly out of the car. Hunched his jacket collar up. Grasped his small revolver with his unsteady hand, and thrust them both into a jacket pocket. Leaned back in through the window and said, "Hotel Borodino."

CHAPTER 20

Y uri was still seething about being sidelined in the data-theft operation when the news came from Moscow: the phone monitoring software was in place — and working. A bugged conversation between Zach and Yolkov was the highlight.

Rudin stiffened as more details came through. "Type up the transcript while they're talking," he told his boys. "Message me something every minute."

"The bug's terrific," he said to Yuri. "Bones has found a Peter Yolkov. Know him?"

Yuri shook his head.

"And an Olga Petrova."

Yuri had to cast his mind back a million years. He found the place he was searching for, and it was no comfort zone. "*Mater Bozh'ye*. Mikhail's girl? Who flew back to Moscow with her mother?" What the hell was she doing in town?

"Has to be the one."

Rudin's cell pinged, and he read the fresh message. "Yolkov's angry about Bones finding out about Petrova." He straightened.

"She's here to kill me."

Yuri laughed. "You have so many well-wishers."

"This kind I don't need more of. She's at Yolkov's." Rudin jabbed at the phone. "Take two guys to this new address," he said to whoever answered. "If Bones is there, bring him here. Don't harm him, much. Find this Yolkov and an Olga. Bring them also, if they don't resist. If they do, then leave them there. Silenced." He closed the call.

"I've been thinking," Yuri said. "A smart secret organization would want you to reveal your base. They might have set this up as bait."

"Crap. The bug's perfect, and they don't know of it." He scrolled back through his messages. "Bones has a surveillance expert looking for me, and anyone who can give him information about me. Let's see who this Yolkov is, and what he thinks he knows." He tapped out new commands to his boys.

"The Petrova girl," Yuri said, "must be twenty now?"

"A dangerous age. They read shit for two seconds, grab a fistful of attitude, then mount their steeds and charge without thought for consequences."

A new message arrived.

Rudin swore. "The Miles bitch She's messaged Bones, telling him of the bug. How the fuck could she know already?"

"The girl Grigor saw. Had to be her."

"She was outside, couldn't hear us talking inside."

"I told you, her organization is very efficient. What if she used a device that penetrated walls?"

Rudin flashed irritation. "No government agency would send their protected person to the home of her suspected abductors. She's unconnected."

"She slipped a bug in through an air vent or something."

"Crap. She guessed a bug existed."

"If any one of them had guessed it, they wouldn't use their phones, would they?"

Rudin glared at him like he was holding stuff back. "So, tell me, genius wizard, what's your next move?"

"I wouldn't do the obvious thing."

"Like go to Yolkov's address and scoop up all these people?"

"It's a trick."

"And if it's not? Any other suggestions, Mr. Mastermind?"

Rudin was falling back on his most tiresome tactic belittling those who tried to help him. Stupid. Only a fool dismissed ideas from a comrade.

"I'm just advising you," Yuri said evenly. "Trying to help."

Rudin tapped his cell. "We should have inserted the software on her phone. Bones will have her on his contact list." He hit more keys to send his boys scurrying to obey him. "The surveillance guy who called Bones? His number also captured. Let's have a listen to him, too."

More instructions flowed from Rudin's fingertips to Moscow. The return message wasn't encouraging.

"Bones isn't talking anymore," Rudin said with exasperation. "They can hear wind and passing cars, but no voices."

"That's it, then," Yuri said. "What's Plan B?"

"Maybe he's dropped the phone and hasn't noticed yet."

"Sure. We wait, and the Good Fairy brings it back."

Rudin ignored him, paced the room, lost in the planning and forecasting of angles, situations, and outcomes. "Our watchers will get to Yolkov's apartment soon. Something will come of that. Bones, Yolkov, Petrova." He counted them off on his fingers.

"One, two, or all of them, will be here later, and most of our problems will evaporate."

The next message told them Keera Miles's phone was now bugged, but she wasn't talking near it. The message after that said the surveillance guy's phone had blocked them.

Yuri said, "They've located the bug, and they're shutting down our access. I told you they were good."

"You know something, Yuri?" Rudin said. "I'm wondering if you should sit out front, and Grigor brews my tea."

Rudin's phone beeped before Yuri thought of any suitable sarcasm.

"*Da*." Rudin listened and nodded with satisfaction. Disconnected. "Three watchers in place," he said. "Nobody at home. We wait, and with luck from above, we'll have all three."

Yolkov had given him Olga's destination hotel. He was weakening. Only enough to help Olga's survival, but he might now spare a moment to think about his.

Zach scrambled out of the car and grabbed his arm. "Be sensible. You can't go home until we remove Rudin from our lives."

Yolkov didn't respond; he only stared at Zach's hand. The old fucker was still preparing to die. Maybe he figured his earlier decision to leave Olga's father's death unavenged had now brought death to Olga. Maybe he was stupidly beating himself up about it. How was he going to get through to this guy?

"We can do this," Zach said. "No need for you to take more risks. Give me a few days to track Rudin down, and we can work out a strategy. I've got a top guy searching already." And Keera, the best human tracker in the world.

Yolkov looked up at him and back at the restraining hand.

"Let me take you to this Hotel Borodino, to Olga. I'll cover the room—hell, you can have a suite if you want—for as long as you need."

"What do I need more time for?" Yolkov said. "I fucked up before, and I've fucked up now. I don't want to feel like this ever again. I don't want to live long enough to see a third time."

"You did what anybody sensible would do, what even I would do, and I'm stupid as a day-old chick. We can bring Rudin down. Time is all we need, and safety for you and Olga, which I can organize."

"You can't organize these thoughts out of my mind, and I can't live with them."

Yolkov wrenched his arm free and walked around the corner. Only a hundred yards to Yolkov's apartment. The guy might get home, but it wouldn't matter. Had to be Russians waiting inside. He moved to the corner building and stepped around it.

Ahead, Yolkov strode with purpose, his gun hand in his pocket. Further ahead, two men emerged from a white van and walked toward him. Two ordinary-looking men, in scrubby white overalls, glancing at the building numbers as if they were searching for the right place to enter and fix somebody's appliance. Nothing unusual going on at all.

Except that Yolkov had drawn his revolver.

One of the men shouted something in a foreign tongue, and they both whipped out handguns. Rudin had readied his men in place, all right. Readied and armed.

Yolkov had made another mistake. The Russians were certainly under orders to bring him in. Rudin would have a critical interest in Yolkov, and the danger he and Olga represented. An execution wasn't in Rudin's interest, but once Yolkov drew his revolver, the situation exploded from caution to pre-emptive strike. He gave the approaching men only one option—shoot first.

The man who had shouted pulled his trigger. Three times, without a pause, holding his gun in one hand, striking a pose. He sprayed every shot.

Yolkov fired back, one hand steadying the other. The first bullet thwacked into the van behind the men; the next one struck the shouter, who doubled up and toppled forward headfirst into the ground.

Zach ran to Yolkov. An instinct he couldn't override.

But it was pointless.

The second man, calmer, methodical, advanced maybe another five yards. He steadied his gun with both hands and fired. Once.

Yolkov dropped softly, like he was too exhausted to carry on.

Another man burst out of the driver's seat, running past the fallen Russian, heading for Zach, who stopped and backed up a few paces.

The second guy grabbed the driver's arm. "*Nyet.*" Pointed to their fallen comrade. The driver retraced his steps and dragged the wounded, moaning Russian to the van. The second guy marched up to Yolkov, inspected the inert body, and sent another bullet into his head.

He raised dark, bleak eyes to Zach. "You, you get in the van."

The Russian was tall, with dark hair. He showed no emotion, no touch of nervousness, and an obvious familiarity with guns and intimidation.

Zach shook his head. "I'm worth more dollars to your Rudin than you can dream of. You shoot me, and he'll shoot you when you tell him what you've done."

He was surprised he could actually speak after all the horror enacted in front of him. There wasn't even a tremor in his voice. He figured the chance of being killed on the spot was negligible. No Zach, no millions for Rudin. Even a wounding was problematical: hospitalization or death the logical outcomes. Both of them unprofitable. The guy wouldn't shoot.

The Russian lifted his gun and pointed it at Zach's head. "Come."

Yolkov lay still on the ground, in a bloody puddle. The direct result of Zach calling him for information. The old guy's life terminated by those who had no regard for it. He owed him something. Resistance, at least. Not an easy submission to the same eventual fate.

He shook his head again.

The Russian said, "I was the top marksman in my unit. I can shoot your ears off, centimeter by centimeter."

"You'll have to."

Through the distant sounds of traffic, a siren wailed in anxious anticipation of what it might find. Across the street, people gathered outside an apartment building to watch. Above them, more faces pressed to glass.

The Russian looked over the sidewalk crowd and back to Zach. He pocketed his gun in his overalls and walked briskly back to the van. He helped to lift the wounded man inside.

Seconds later, the van sped to the end of the street and around the corner. Zach memorized the license number but knew it wouldn't help. These people killed for a living. They

wouldn't mess up the small stuff.

CHAPTER 21

When the cops arrived, the crowd thickened and the officers pput up crime scene tape. Zach identified himself to the uniforms that approached, explained he was a witness to the shooting, and that he knew the victim. Said he'd wait right there for the detectives to arrive.

A pair of detectives showed up, and one of them introduced himself to Zach while the other interviewed any onlooker who had a story to tell.

Zach delivered the basic details of the event, descriptions of the men, definitely not tradespeople, and the lvan's license plate. Explained why he was with Yolkov: routine background interview about data theft.

"Why were you walking so far behind the victim?" asked Detective Sergeant Witold Kolacz.

"He said to drop him at the corner." Zach seeing the same moment again in his mind: the moment he should have kept driving. "After he got out, I remembered something I wanted to ask, and followed him around the corner, then the nightmare.

Jesus." His story didn't sound good; sounded like he knew an ambush lay ahead and had stood back.

"He wanted to walk the last hundred yards alone?" Kolacz asked. "He say why?"

"No. I assume he didn't want to be seen with a reporter."

"You said he was also a reporter, but he didn't want to be seen with another one. Sounds funny to me. You got a better explanation?" The detective lowered his notebook.

Here it comes, the cop attitude, unrolling like a bale of barbed wire. "That's what he told me. I mean, he was giving me information about Russian organized crime. Not a lot, but enough to make a man paranoid. He wasn't wrong, was he?"

"Any Russian in particular?"

"A Dmitri Rudin. Apparently a big shot in Brooklyn, been seen around our little town. Data theft is his main passion."

"You think he's connected to the City Hall data hack?"

"Let me see. Data theft guy in town, data breach at City Hall. Hmm, sounds like a connection."

Kolacz said, "The theft of personal data does not require the presence of the thief in the same town. You know that?"

"In my business, like yours, Detective, we chase connections to see what pops up."

"But unlike your business, Bones, we actually perform a public service."

"Most of the time."

Kolacz darkened. "Are you disparaging the Chicago Police Department?"

Jesus. Yolkov lying there, a small huddled mass under a blue sheet, and the detective wants respect. Wants his status noticed and duly noted, and tough Twinkies to the poor stiff who deserved a better ending than two hot bullets on a cold sidewalk.

"Disparaging?" Zach said. "No. Just striving for accuracy in our conversation."

"Accuracy, exactly what I want in your replies to my questions. Opinions, they're not so useful. They should be kept to yourself unless I ask for them."

"Sorry, I'm not thinking straight. Observing killings at close range is not normally how I spend my day. Can we please get on with the questions? I have other people to see."

Kolacz didn't seem so convinced of Zach's fragile mental state, but he didn't ride him any further. He checked his notebook.

"Zachary Bones. Of the *Chicago Post*," Kolacz said. "You a crime reporter?"

"I cover local politics. But sometimes I catch another kind of story, and I get to run with it."

"You ever run with a Russian story before?"

The question he didn't want. The question that would open a whole new line of investigation and shake his credibility. He couldn't fudge it either. Once his name was entered in the police database, Kolacz would discover the Vronsky killing six months earlier. With him and Keera at the scene.

"In a way," he said. "Me and my girlfriend were once the victims of an attempted hold-up by a Russian guy who, amazingly, was shot dead by a couple of other Russians on the spot. A turf war, the local police said."

Kolacz folded his arms. "Amazingly, you say. I'd use another adverb myself."

"That event had nothing to do with this one. I wasn't chasing a story, nothing. This mugger comes up, and then *blam-blam*, he gets taken out by other bad guys. Worst day of my life."

Kolacz smiled like this story was the best ever. "The day is yet young."

"It happened in Old Town," Zach said. "Check the local precinct." The place where he'd tried to register a missing person report when Keera was kidnapped. More unusual stuff for Kolacz to wonder about. Highly suspicious stuff.

The detective opened his notebook, scribbled again.

"You dropped the vic off? Where's your car?" he asked.

"Around the corner."

"Makes sense. Wouldn't want it wearing any bullet holes."

The detective couldn't have made his thoughts any more obvious if he'd bought advertising space during the Super Bowl.

Zach led Kolacz back to his car. "What, exactly, are you inferring?"

"I'm wondering if you have psychic powers. Lots of people have them. The city's full of those types."

Kolacz wrote down his license number and asked for the car's paperwork. As Zach opened the door to retrieve the papers from the glovebox, faint dance music sounded from the trunk.

"What's that?" Kolacz asked.

"Um, my phone."

"In the trunk? Open it."

Zach opened it and the electro beats grew louder.

"I can't see any phone," Kolacz said.

Zach unraveled the blanket as the music stopped. The phone lay there, inert and accusing.

Kolacz said, "You always ride around with your phone in the trunk, wrapped up in a blanket?"

"It's a personal idiosyncrasy. Most people find it charming."

Detective Kolacz snapped his notebook shut. "I'm going to ask around about you, and I don't know why, but I have a feeling we're going to talk again. Does that suit you? Because if it doesn't, I don't give a shit."

When Kolacz had left, Zach covered up his phone and slammed the trunk lid shut. He retrieved his old phone, now half-charged, from the car. Plenty was sure to have the antidote to any software bugging.

He called him. Got voicemail. "My phone's bugged," he said, assuming Plenty would recognize his voice. That his photographic memory was working. "Please send me the fix. Also my partner's." He gave her number, and as an afterthought added his current number. "It's urgent. Fucking urgent. One man dead already."

He cut the connection and leaned against his car. What he'd said to Kolacz about the Vronsky killing being the worst day of his life? Wrong. This was.

Yolkov dead because he agreed to meet Zach. A guy who had no interest in Zach's story, no dog in the fight against Rudin until this Olga knocked on his door. And without Zach's involvement, Olga's idea would have gone nowhere: Rudin would have remained hidden. The two of them left to consume their bitterness in vodka, to realize their dreams were pointless, and Olga returning home. Now, Yolkov was dead, and Olga destined to join him. Within days.

His phone chirped. "It's me," Plenty said. "Don't talk. Reboot the phones you mentioned, and all's well." He cut off.

Zach carried out Plenty's instructions, noticing that it was Keera who had just called him and inadvertently antagonized Kolacz further. He sent her a text to reboot her phone and to text him back when she was done. He didn't mention Yolkov.

There had to be an appropriate way to announce he'd caused the death of an innocent man. Some protocol he could follow that buffered the pain. But he couldn't think of one.

Another thing they didn't teach him at journalism school.

Keera opened her laptop and map-searched for the pink house. Found the street in Highland Park; the photo of the house showing it more worn than today. The owners must have spruced it up for the incoming occupants.

She clicked on the Directions icon. A jagged line linked her house to the pink house. Only fifteen minutes away, if she wanted to drive there.

And Zach would. As soon as he got back. She'd have to dissuade him. That Grigor was receptive enough to spot her flitting about again. The one problem they hadn't predicted—Rudin had a psychic guard. Not that he knew it.

She guessed, judging by her experience with Russians, Grigor was rarely without vodka in his system. If you harried those with psychic powers, distracted them, or dulled their abilities with alcohol or other chemicals foreign to the body, their gifts were useless.

A shape drifted across her line of sight. Donnie.

"You again," she said.

"Yep," he said. "Don't mean to bust in like this but you oughta know that your boyfriend's walking into a shitstorm."

"Zach? How? Where?" She pressed her hands on the table to still them.

"You know he's mixing with the wrong people."

No shit. "What's the problem?" She fought to keep her voice level. There's no mileage in shouting at spooks.

"There's foreigners pointing guns at him."

What! "Quick, how can I help?"

Donnie smiled ruefully like there was nothing she could do but wait. Like he only now realized that you don't come to the physical plane to freak people out. You appear when you're able to help. She wanted to yell at him to make sure he understood, but the way he was fading from view made it clear he'd got the message as soon as she'd thought of it.

Dammit, Donnie.

Thoughts of Zach drifted across her mind, accompanied by forebodings with darker ideas trailing behind them. What was he doing? Where was he? Not knowing any of the answers she needed produced more anxiety.

She picked up her phone. Bugged or not, she had to hear his voice to steady herself. She knew what was affecting her. Not an idle thought that grew and fed upon itself until strong enough to throw her into a panic; it was something more tangible.

Zach was scared. Scared enough for his terror to project itself across the city and find her. She jabbed at the screen and gripped the phone tightly while she listened to his phone ring and ring until she couldn't bear it anymore and switched off.

He'd been shocked by her revelation about his phone and had disconnected without saying why. He hadn't had to. Names, maybe addresses had been compromised. Not theirs, or he would have alerted her to flee. That left the obvious victims. Yolkov. Olga.

Her phone buzzed the incoming text alert, and her heart lifted as she read it. The reboot he had demanded took a slow century to complete while she waited to text Zach back. Finally. *RU OK? Talk to me.*

When she heard his voice, she almost burst into tears. His wasn't the jokey, good-timey voice she knew; what came across the speaker was tight, strained, and clipped.

"Yolkov's dead," he said.

Prepared as she was, the straight-out confirmation rocked her. "Because of the bugging?"

"Because of the bugging. Olga's missing. Might be safe, might be caught. I have to find out."

"Please come home," she begged.

"This won't take long. What does she look like?"

"Tell me you're not hurt."

Zach took his time to reply. "Not hurt, no visible wounds. All the serious damage is mental."

"Olga is tall and very white, white-blonde hair as well. Blue eyes, and a snappy way about her. Love you," she added, surprising herself.

"Love you too, always will. I'll call soon."

"You have to. Waiting and not knowing is the most painful thing I've ever endured."

Later she calmed herself with her chamomile tea, allowed thoughts to flicker into life and fade until her mind achieved the tranquility it needed.

That Zach would try to save Olga wasn't in question; where he would find her was another matter. The white van floated across her mind, and she fastened on it. The van speeding along a main road, three men inside. No Olga. One man lying in the back, on a mattress, and clutching his stomach, blood seeping through fingers, his strength ebbing. The man in the passenger seat watching him. All of them armed, the wounded man's gun covered in blood. A feeling grew he wouldn't survive. What that meant for Zach, she didn't want to dwell on.

Zach hadn't mentioned a gun battle—a gun battle, for God's sake. It explained the way he'd sounded. His adrenaline levels off the scale during the worst moments, and the immediate aftermath. The inner turmoil he was suffering, she couldn't measure.

CHAPTER 22

Zach stabbed at the ignition slot several times before the key slid home. The killing and the near-death experience at the hand of the Russian had left him shaky as shit. He called Plenty and outlined the disaster the day had become.

"I'm dealing with people who are more murderous than I expected," he said. "I'm out of my depth."

"You need more protection," Plenty said. "I can supply bodyguards, but they won't die for you if they face an armed attack. No offense, Zach, but you're not that important to them or the nation."

"Love your reassurance."

"But we can ramp up intelligence. Get advance warning of any hostile move."

He already had Keera. What could Plenty provide that she couldn't?

"If you can supply their phone numbers," Plenty said, "I can bug them like they bugged you. The latest version even supplies the GPS coordinates."

"I only have Sidirov's, and he's just a messenger boy. They won't include him in their planning."

"Let me try. I can get to his contacts list."

Zach gave him the number.

"If I discover anything big," Plenty said, "I'll text you a single word—*Roy.* That means to call me when youcan talk freely."

"Like spy-meets-spy stuff?"

"You smirk, but I have to know others aren't listening. These guys are no amateurs." Plenty closed the connection.

Zach keyed Hotel Borodino into his map app, and the GPS displayed the shortest route to the next hell. Keera had described Olga as snappy. She wouldn't stay that way after he told her about Yolkov. Probably go all weepy and dramatic. Have to be helped to the car and driven to Lake Forest.

Wait. The house was *their* haven, not Olga's. She owed no allegiance him or Keera. She was likely to blame Zach for Yolkov's death; she might even rat them out to Rudin for the chance to get close enough to kill him. The way Keera had explained it that night, Olga wasn't one to care about her death —she was fixated on Rudin's. But she couldn't stay at the hotel either. Her ID now lived on its database, and available online for anyone who knew how to find it. Which Rudin's men did.

There was no alternative. Olga was to be a house guest for the time being, which would work—if she didn't know where she was.

The Hotel Borodino presented well on the outside. Fresh paint, golden touches to the Victorian facade perked the building up even further. But a hotel named after an epic and victorious Russian battle with Napoleon was not the best choice for a Russian girl hiding out.

Inside, any idea of a further makeover had died in the decorator's mind. Faded brown carpets and walls. All the doors leading off the lobby wore scuff marks at their bases. Maybe the clientele liked to kick doors open. Maybe they walked into them. The receptionist didn't look too sharp, either.

"I've come for an Olga," he said to the part-Asiatic guy behind the counter. His name badge read Timur, and Zach guessed he was originally from the far eastern reaches of Siberia. Must have hated Chicago, except for the constant hot water, the astonishing range of food choices, exemplary medical services, and availability of young women interested in young foreign guys.

"Do you have room number?" Timur asked.

"Just Olga is all I know. I'm giving her a lift to a friend's place."

Timur checked his screen, picked up a phone, murmured into it. Then had to murmur a bunch more because it appeared Olga wasn't coming down just like that. You didn't need to be a psychologist to know that her personality was mostly contrarian. She didn't take orders or suggestions lightly.

Timur replaced the handset. "Olga here soon."

Like hell.

He should have made up some credible story, not walked in and expected a smooth result. He checked his GPS, enlarged the screen image, and located the rear of the hotel.

"I have to move my car," he said the clerk. "I'll be back in a minute."

Timur nodded, blank-faced, busied himself with inspecting his pen for blemishes.

Zach drove his car around the block and slowed to a cruise. No sign of any Olga. Nothing. He cicled again. This time—bingo.

A tall woman ahead, white-blond hair, red scarf catching the breeze, wheeling a suitcase behind her. Zach pulled up beside her. She looked around and froze.

He stepped out and said, "I'm Zach Bones. Yolkov is dead. Rudin's men shot him. They're looking for you. Please get in."

Olga didn't move. Who could blame her? He tried again. "Today, this morning, Yolkov told me about you. He knew he would die. You're in danger, you have to come. Now."

Not a muscle of hers moved, if you didn't count blinking. Zach wondered if she knew any English. "Look how quickly I found you. Yolkov gave me the hotel name, asked me to protect you. Rudin's men will locate you within the hour. Your hotel registration is already online, and his men will be searching for it. Please get in."

Her eyes flicked up the street, then down. Twice. She understood English.

"See what you just did?" Zach said. "You checked the street for any threats. You'll be doing that for the rest of your life if you don't come with me. I'm the only friend you have in town."

Still, she didn't move. Jesus. Fucking get in the car. "I will help you find Rudin," he added.

That was a downright lie. The only plan he had in mind for Olga was to send her back to Russia. But lies work, which was the best reason to use them. She pointed to her suitcase, like he was a cabbie, and took the passenger seat while he loaded her case into the trunk.

"Where did they kill him?" she asked as they drew away from the curb. Her English pronunciation was a stilted product of language school.

"Outside his apartment. They were waiting for him."

"They didn't take him away?"

"He pulled out a gun and shot one of them, so they killed him."

Still no reaction. They made them stoic in Russia.

"They didn't kill you?" she said. "Why?"

"They need me alive and in good health."

"Lucky man. Why?"

"They think they can make money out of me."

"Why?"

"Did they teach you other words in language school? In this country, asking about private matters is not good manners."

She turned to him, and he was startled to see wet eyes.

"Good manners, yes. We have them also. But good manners will not bring Yolkov back."

"Or your father." He hadn't meant to reveal he knew this, it sounded callous in the moment.

She turned away from him. "You know so much. Why?"

That damn word again. Olga would drive him crazy by nightfall. "I'll answer your questions later. Right now, I want you to take off your scarf. And don't ask me why."

"Of course I have to ask this, your request is silly one."

"Please wrap it around your eyes so you can't see where I'm taking you. It's for your safety and ours."

She surprised him by not pushing back. The scarf was thick, and after she'd wound it several times around her head, she was effectively blind. The blindfold added the surprising benefit of making her fall silent until they swept through the gates at Lake Forest.

◆ ◆ ◆

180

By late afternoon Yuri was tired of listening to Dmitri Rudin. First, the guy was pleased his watchers were in place on Yolkov's street so fast.

"We have good people here," Rudin said with evident satisfaction. "They know what to do."

Then he was spitting fury because Bones had escaped.

"He's the whole reason we're here," Rudin shouted when the watchers returned and reported.

The news of the shooting and subsequent death of a watcher hardly grazed his consciousness, and Yolkov's extinction elicited only a brief grunt of satisfaction. What made Rudin most angry was Olga's disappearance.

"Of all the targets," he thundered at the room, "she was the easiest, the most unprotected. A little girl."

"I told you," Yuri said, "Bones has a good organization behind him. Once they picked up the phone bug, they moved fast to protect their people. If this Olga was of interest to them, then they took her to safety."

"Such safety," Rudin snapped. "My boys located her in the hotel an hour after she checked in. This mysterious organization is extremely stupid."

"Bait. She was bait. Waiting for more of us to come after her and get wiped out."

"Which didn't happen. Bones came to her location, and she skipped. Didn't leave with him, as we know."

Yuri spread his palms. "A change of plans, maybe."

"The Bones guy," Lev said from the couch, "wasn't protected at all. I had my pistol on him, close enough to ask him which ear did he want to lose first. I could have terminated him right there."

"Good thing you stayed sensible," Rudin said, thin-lipped. "He's worth a lot to us."

To us? To Rudin, was more like it. "What did he say?" Yuri asked Lev. "When you mentioned his ears?"

"He said I'd have to shoot them off. He wasn't going to the van."

"You see," Yuri said triumphantly. "He knew he had back-up. Guys with rifles, just itching to blast craters in you."

"Any back-up crew would have opened fire as soon as I lifted the pistol. Your theory is bullshit." Lev bent down and rubbed a stain on his shoe. "Your opinions are highly valued, of course, but you notice the people we want are still running free. They didn't do this by themselves."

Rudin said, "Much of what you say, Yuri, makes sense. The way they discovered the bug, the way they removed Olga, twice. The girl Grigor saw at the gate. The way Bones wasn't worried about Lev. But they don't operate like any known government unit. All I know is Olga is important to them, and us. That's why we have to find her."

"You're not worried anymore that she'll try to kill you?"

"There's that, of course. But she should be easier to crack than Bones, and tell us about the people behind them."

"You don't listen to the message they are sending us," Yuri said. "They are saying if we leave Bones and the girl alone, they'll be happy. All the signs point to it."

"What signs?"

"They could have taken out the van with three men inside. And they didn't."

"Like how? With a grenade launcher? A bomb? In the middle of a big city? And bring down every fucking government agency, and the world's media, on their heads? Don't be stupid."

Rudin was impossible. The facts laid out in front him, arranged neatly on a plate, and still he ignored them. Yuri tried one more time. "I bet they know where we are right now. We ought to leave town, try again later."

Rudin said, "You think I'd walk away from an open pot of gold. This is the most exciting opportunity since banks were invented."

The front door opened and closed. A thick farmhand of a man walked in. Konstantin, a van driver when required, semi-lethal muscle at other, more physical times.

"You take care of body, no problem?" Rudin asked.

"The body," Lev said flatly, "has a name and a family."

"I apologize," Rudin said. "I was thinking of logistics, and I forgot to pay proper respect. It's important everything is tidy before authorities knock on door."

"The funeral director," Konstantin said, "has arranged for the correct papers, and the casket will fly to Moscow tonight. The family has been informed, the van is spotless, the plates changed."

"Good work," Rudin said. "I'll arrange appropriate compensation for the family later."

Probably a couple of free tickets to the Bolshoi Ballet, Yuri thought.

Rudin must have caught a whiff of his thoughts because he addressed him sharply. "The usual compensation is twice the last year's income. His family will not be left wanting."

"It's a very generous benefit," Yuri agreed, but Rudin gave him the cold eye anyway.

A new sound intruded—high-pitched buzzing. They stared at

the ceiling as if it was responsible.

"A police chopper," Yuri said.

"The fuck it is," Rudin barked. "Sounds like bees."

"If you hadn't dodged military service, Yuri," Lev said, "you'd know it's no chopper."

The buzzing drew closer, louder, lower, outside in the driveway. They focused on the front door.

It shook from a thud, then another. A giant's knock.

A single gunshot.

Silence.

CHAPTER 23

Zach introduced Olga, tall, blonde, imperious, to Keera, six inches shorter , dark-haired, and tense.

Olga inspected her surroundings as if expecting something better. Keera led them into the living area where she made tea, black with lemon for Olga, chamomile for herself. Zach made his own coffee.

With the Russian girl present, Zach had to limit what he told Keera. He started with a shot-by-shot account of the gun battle. Olga didn't react to a word of it. She didn't even soften when he described how Yolkov had given him the hotel details, knowing he was about to die. But she did, at least, nod agreement when Zach revealed how he'd convinced her to go with him.

When he finished, Keera said, "I have news as well."

Zach narrowed his eyes to signal that Olga, too young and too crazy with revenge, couldn't be trusted with any important information.

Keera got it. "Our contact came through. Rudin's behind the data heist."

"How about that, who would've thought it?"

"Also, our contact has his address—"

"Where is he?" Olga exclaimed. "Tell me."

"Not so fast," Zach said. "We're dealing with very dangerous people here. Every step we take, we plan it out first."

"What's to plan? I knock on door, ask to see him, then *pow pow,* big bullets in face."

Jesus Christ. Just the loose cannon they needed. "You have a gun?" he asked.

"No, but they are easy to buy here. Everybody knows this."

"You won't get past the door guard. He'll frisk you."

"What is this frisk?"

"He'll feel all over your body, searching for a weapon. Even then, he'll wait for orders before you're allowed in. I know how secretive this Rudin is. And since they're looking for you, all you'll be doing is giving yourself up. Your death will follow shortly."

Olga sneered. "Any guard touching my body will feel my anger. I have top training in martial arts. I cripple him with one kick."

He should have left her on the street. Starvation was safer than what she wanted to pursue. "Here's the plan," he said. "We tackle this two ways. First, we let Rudin know we have located him."

"How will you do that?" Keera asked in such a calm way he knew she suspected foolishness.

"I'll drop him my calling card."

"And then?"

"He'll rush back to Brooklyn."

"Your enthusiasm is not infectious," she said.

"Wait, there's more. I'll interview Olga about her mission to discover her father's killer, and suggest Rudin may be involved. When this is published, Rudin will act. Most likely he'll find a new hideaway before the police come with their pesky questions. A further story will provide persuasive evidence of Rudin connected to the data theft. Yolkov's killing, while he was revealing Rudin's background, adds more weight to my story."

"You think he'll be so busy saving his skin, he'll forget about us."

"Pretty much," he said.

Olga said, "How can I find him if he hides again?"

"If you find him," Zach said, "you'll give him the chance to kill you as well as your father. Go home."

"If I go home, he will find me faster than here. I will be dead person when I land." She stood. "Please show me to my room."

Keera took her upstairs and returned.

"Where do you find these delightful people?" she asked.

"They are called story sources—the lifeblood of my career."

"Glad they're not mine."

"What's Rudin's address?"

She told him and described her encounter with the partly psychic guard. "How are you delivering your card? I wouldn't recommend knocking on the door."

"I'm airmailing it," Zach said.

Zach drove to an electronics store and examined a small drone in a line-up of much larger ones.

"How far will this drone fly?" he asked the sales clerk.

She was in her early twenties, brown-skinned and softly spoken. Her name badge said Priya.

"It's not a drone," she said. "That's a plane without a pilot; this is a multi-rotor. As it has four propellers, so it's called a quadcopter."

Like I cared. "How far will it fly?" he asked again.

"This one has a range of four hundred yards and about a hundred feet of altitude. If you fly it past those parameters, it automatically returns to the control unit. Flight time is ten minutes."

Zach figured four hundred yards should be enough.

Priya must have assumed she was talking over his head, might lose a sale. "Your choice is way cool," she said.

"That's important. I also want a camera to attach to it."

"It's already got one. Unless you're planning to work for *National Geographic,* you should choose another model. The lens resolution is not designed for high-quality images. Bad news for those who like to spy on their neighbors."

"Hate those guys. I want to clip something to it."

"How heavy?"

"A business card."

"You a real estate guy?"

"Something more boring."

"If you're talking about a release mechanism, then we don't have such things. They'll be expensive, maybe more than this unit."

Since Keera hadn't objected to spending the dirty money to outwit Rudin, he figured he might as well scrifice the hundred-buck quadcopter when it delivered the card.

Priya said, "This also has a cute fly-around-me function."

"Would I like it?"

"Takes selfies of you from up high."

"Sold."

"Batteries are extra," she said. "You'll find them next to the checkout."

Zach didn't take the chance of being spotted in his recognizable Mustang by driving along Rudin's street. He circled the adjoining streets toward the pink house, looking for a white van parked to spot an approching enemy. Like him.

The quadcopter needed assembling, but the nice people at the factory had included a toy screwdriver to attach the toy propeller blades. He wedged his card in the assembled machine. He set it going, and played with the control unit, maneuvering the joystick up and down, and steering the quadcopter along the street to get the hang of it. Worked as advertised. Loud as a small lawnmower.

Nearby, the front door of a house flew open, and a senior citizen emerged and marched up to him. "You fly that contraption over my place," the guy said, "and I'll kick every panel on your car till it looks like the Seven Dwarfs used it for hammering practice."

"Relax," Zach said to his florid face. "Just a prank on a pal. I'll keep a respectful distance from your home."

"Make sure you do," the guy muttered, and marched back to his door and took up a watchful station.

Zach guided the contraption up high and shifted it away from the angry guy's place. Edged it west until he spotted the pink house on the screen. Priya was right: the picture quality was shitty, but he could distinguish between colors. A black SUV and a white van were parked in the driveway.

He reduced altitude over Rudin's street, and came in over his gated driveway, the guard visible. The guard shaded his eyes with one hand, looked up, and drew a gun from his waistband. Zach slowed speed and dropped the quadcopter to chest height. Headed for the front door. Past the guard who did nothing.

He was now so low he couldn't see far ahead and prayed the flight path was correct. It was. The quadcopter rammed the door and bounced back, the screen displaying jerky visuals of the front door area, still flying, for God's sake. How good was that?

Zach pushed the joystick forward again, and the flying machine responded with another thump into the door. His screen showed door, walls, windows zooming across it, and he guessed the unit was mortally wounded, and out of control.

When he saw the guard on the screen, with the gun pointed directly at the drone, he was sure of it.

The screen blacked out.

A street away, a single gunshot spooked birds out of trees.

Lev was the first through the front door, his gun out, finger outside the trigger guard. Grigor had his weapon aimed at a black chunk of plastic on the ground. Smaller pieces lay scattered around.

"One of those drone things," Grigor said. "Whoever sent it, has to be close. I'll look around."

"Wait," Yuri said. "This could be a trap." Guys with guns and muscles never understood a complex scenario.

Rudin bent over the wreckage, extracted a business card. Glanced at the front. *Zachary Bones. Journalist. The Chicago Post.* A phone number and an email address. He flipped it over to check the back. *Greetings, Dmitri Rudin.*

"It's that prick, Bones."

"What's his problem?" Yuri asked. "He doesn't like the color of front door?"

"You think this amusing? He's discovered us. And he now knows my last name."

"More likely it's his government pals. Bones is only messenger."

"Why aren't they busting in through every door and window, with flash bombs and automatics?"

"We have broken no laws here. We suggested a business proposal to a local citizen. America is in favor of such things."

"So they just watch?" Rudin flipped the card front to back as if to unearth a hidden meaning.

"They're signaling," Yuri said. "They want us to know they're watching. They'd rather we leave than have to arrest us."

Rudin said, "I expect muscle, guns fired maybe. But a drone? With card?"

"The card is message. And Bones has a childish sense of humor, which explains delivery method. The question is, what will they do if we don't leave?"

"If they meant to arrive with warrants, they would've done it by now. We're safe here for now." Rudin lifted his chin at Lev. "You and Konstantin circle the area, look out for an old red Mustang."

Grigor activated the gates, and the two of them reversed the van down the driveway and roared off to the hunt.

"This drone," Grigor said, "came in low, didn't fly over and check out the place, just bashed into door. Twice. I saw box under it and, thinking it might be bomb, I shot the crap out of it."

"You didn't see the card sticking up?" Yuri asked.

"I thought it was price tag."

"The box was not a bomb, it was a camera. The operator can't navigate without it."

Rudin kicked at the wrecked drone. "Is this thing still videoing us? Or listening?"

"I can make sure," Grigor said, aiming his gun.

"No. No more gunshots. If police come now, we explain shooting down of illegal surveillance craft on our property. It was close to ground, and nobody was in danger of being hit with bullet. Your weapon is legal, registered, no trouble there. But more shooting, cops are suspicious. For now, wrap up all this in plastic bag and keep it away from us."

Grigor walked inside.

Yuri asked, "How long before we find Bones and his girlfriend?"

"Faster than you know. You can't even think without leaving a trace."

"From what Sidirov told us, he's backed out of the deal, so he must be ready for us to renew acquaintance."

Rudin threw a deliberate look at the drone remains and Yuri shut up. When Grigor returned with his bag, they moved back inside.

"The way I see it," Yuri said. "He's got the million he promised us. Now he's keeping it because he feels insulted he wasn't treated as an equal."

Rudin said, "Wounded by truth, was he? Poor soul."

"The problem is that he can spend that money to solve his problem with us."

"Like buying a flying toy?"

"It wasn't cheap. Maybe two hundred dollars."

Rudin laughed. "He can afford thousands of them. We'll have

much entertainment."

"He can do more than provide entertainment now he has our location."

"Nothing illegal. He has to obey the law."

"When you have a million, you don't have to obey everybody."

"What are you saying?"

Yuri said, "He can hire people to wait until we're all in car, fly a drone up to it, rest it gently on roof and detonate small bomb. Vaporize us."

Rudin stared at him. "Surely not. He's a crusading reporter."

"As a great leader once said, 'Any man will abandon his principles to save his life.'"

"Who was that?"

"I can't recall."

"Then he wasn't a great leader."

"He may have been a lesser one."

"*Mater Bozh'ye*," Rudin said. "I need a drink."

CHAPTER 24

Keera spread her academic folders on the dining table. She flipped open her laptop, emailed the students waiting to consult with her, telling them a family emergency was keeping her at home, but she'd contact them personally over the next few days.

That was assuming Zach didn't bait the Russian bear in his cave past endurance. Such a reckless idea to send a drone to them with his calling card. But bless the guy for enjoying his work, even if it put him at greater risk.

Olga appeared at the door: jeans, short leather jacket, shoulder bag. Keera hadn't heard her descend the stairs.

"You're so quiet," Keera said.

"Yes. Game we played when I was young: to see who was quietest when sneaking up on each other. Also, who was best at hiding. I always won."

How fascinating. "You hungry?" Keera asked. "There are snacks in the fridge." Meaning, help yourself, lady, I'm not serving you.

Olga glided over and found yogurt and soda. Teenage food:

half health, half sugar. Joined Keera at the table.

"What are these papers?" she asked.

"I am an assistant professor, I'm helping students with their final papers for the year."

"What is subject?"

"Anthropology."

"Ah, you investigate dead people?" Olga spooned yogurt into her mouth with brisk efficiency.

"Well, yes. Sometimes, centuries after they die."

"How did Yolkov know Rudin's men were waiting for him?"

Here comes the interrogation, the suspicious, wild-eyed version. The part where Olga won't believe anything I say. "We were warned Rudin was listening to Zach and had discovered Yolkov's address. Zach told him right away. For some reason, he refused to avoid them."

She pondered on this long enough to finish the yogurt and drain the soda. She glanced at the fridge.

"Help yourself if you're still hungry," Keera said. "I'll text Zach to bring more food."

She moved items around in the fridge and emerged with a beer. Checked out the food cupboards and selected a bag of corn chips. How sweet. Now I have two chip-crunching, beer-swiggers in the house.

Olga resumed her place at the table and crushed a chip loud enough to frighten a horse. "When," she asked, "do we visit Rudin and kill him?"

"The thing is," Keera said, "in this country, we leave the legal killing of citizens to the government."

"What does your government do about revenge? Honorable, necessary revenge?"

195

"It's not recognized as a legal activity. Prove Rudin killed your father and the police will do the rest."

"Hah." Olga unscrewed the beer top and took a well-practiced swig.

"What we are doing, Olga, is collecting enough evidence to get rid of Rudin and hopefully to have him arrested."

"Hah."

"This is where you can help. When Zach returns, he'll talk to you and write a story for his newspaper. We're hoping to link Rudin to your father's death."

Olga tinkled her fingernails against the beer bottle. "Why is Rudin interested in your Zach?"

Zach hadn't mentioned whether this issue had arisen earlier with Olga. She kept her answer as vague as possible. "We were both involved with Rudin's associates some time ago. It ended badly for them, and Rudin thinks we have a pile of money that belongs to him. We don't, but he doesn't believe us."

"Hah."

"What does that mean?" Olga was getting seriously irksome, and Keera regretted telling her even as much as she had.

"I have come here to avenge my father's death, and all you care about is money. That is why I say, 'hah.'"

Keera placed both hands on the table to stop them from crushing Olga's windpipe. "You are wrong. This is how it is: if we don't remove Rudin from our lives, then all three of us will die. That's all you have to remember. If we keep our common interest in the front of our minds, we will succeed. Please don't tell me your motivation is more important than ours. It isn't."

"How is it," Olga asked, "that a professor like you is interested in my father and me?"

"Assistant professor. I'm helping Zach to remove Rudin from his life, which requires investigations into Rudin's activities. His suspected killing of your father came to light."

"Yolkov told you this?"

"We knew already, Yolkov confirmed it."

Olga munched through the rest of the chips without a response. Keera wanted to cover her ears. "Keep in mind," she said, "when you decide to punish Rudin and his men, that Yolkov has killed one of them already. They will be angry and seek revenge, like you." Olga screwed up the empty chip bag. God, it was loud.

"How you know he killed this man?"

The questions would keep coming, and sooner or later Olga would sense she was being fed a bunch of lies and half-truths. Her confidence in them was minimal already, and any further evidence that made her believe she was being manipulated could be disastrous.

"I can't tell you how we know, but we do," Keera said. "Journalists work with a lot of sources, and they are often confidential. Even the police cannot make you reveal them. If you knew who it was, it would be dangerous for you."

"The police have no power to ask?" Olga surprised at this.

"It's the law."

"They don't beat you anyway?"

"Sometimes, but only if you come from the lower economic classes." She felt like a traitor admitting this to a foreigner but knew police attitudes were similar in most countries.

Olga finished her beer and pushed the empty away. "How much food is Zach bringing? I am trained athlete; I have to keep my strength at peak levels."

"And I have some work to complete. If I arrange for more nourishment, can I have a moment to concentrate on my papers?" If that sounded cold, Keera was beyond caring. Olga was a self-centered child, oblivious to the effect she had on others. The sooner they packed her onto a Moscow flight, the better. There was something dangerous about the girl, something Keera couldn't pin down; no visions appeared, no clear sense of what lay ahead, except that a growing certainty that Olga would provoke a brutal confrontation.

Bodies. Keera saw bodies on the ground.

"Yes," Olga said agreeably. "You do paperwork, and I will wait for your Zach to bring provisions." She pulled out a phone and played fingers over the screen. Looked up again. "Where can I purchase weapons at good price?"

The girl had no more sense than her packet of chips. "Let me tell you something," Keera said. "The minute you point a gun at one of these criminals, you will guarantee your own death."

"I know that. Where can I get gun?"

◆ ◆ ◆

Zach caught Keera's text as he sped out of Highland Park before the Russians managed to circle the block and grab him.

Bring back beer and chips for our athletic guest.

Sounded like Olga was annoying Keera again. Worse, she was drinking his beer. He turned south to the nearest Trader Joe's. If this Rudin business became a long-term situation, he'd better stock up with quality fare. He messaged back telling her the card delivery had been successful, and he was on the way home.

The atmosphere at the house was just above zero when he arrived. Keera flushed out a container of chocolate-covered macadamia nuts from the shopping bags and retreated to a pile of paperwork on the dining table. A clear signal she wouldn't be chatty anytime soon.

Olga examined the three varieties of corn chips he'd bought and nodded with approval. Two six-packs found shelves in the fridge, with one bottle retained for Olga's immediate use.

"Story time," he told her. "Can we talk now?"

Olga lifted a shoulder which he assumed meant yes, I guess, I don't know.

"Use the study," Keera said, pointing out the door without looking up.

Zach led Olga to it, and she moved fast to take the chair behind the desk. When she opened and closed all the drawers, he interjected. "In this country, we don't pry," he said. "It's not polite."

"I was looking for listening device, dangerous things as we know."

"Nothing like that in here, but I'm taping this interview," he said. "To make sure I don't misquote you." Olga shrugged like she didn't care what the hell he misquoted.

Zach switched on his cell recorder. "This is the way I plan to lay out the story. Young Olga arrives in the USA to urge the authorities to reopen the case of her father slain ten years ago."

"Young? I am twenty-two years old."

"No problem, I'll put down your age, and the readers can make up their own minds about your youth. She meets Yolkov here in Chicago who knows of the matter, and who suggests that Dmitri Rudin may have knowledge of it as well. Coincidentally, Rudin is in town at the same time. Within days, Yolkov is gunned down in the street—"

Big tears rolled down her face. She brushed them away with the back of her hand and drank more beer.

"By some miracle," he continued, "Olga leaves the apartment to go shopping and escapes the killers. She is now in hiding, in fear of her life—"

"I am not afraid of anybody. Don't make me look like a quivering jellyfish."

"Okay, I won't say, 'in fear of your life.'"

"I am not in hiding either. I am organizing matters to deliver justice."

"What if I say, Olga is pressing on undeterred, determined to bring justice to her father's killer?"

"Is better like I said it."

"Only if you want people laughing at you."

She compressed her lips but didn't press the matter.

He continued. "The same day, there is a data breach at City Hall. Rudin is known to have links with data thieves and police are investigating." He had no idea if this was true, but it didn't hurt to tell the cops what to do.

"Pictures," he said. "Pictures of you and Yolkov. Do you have any?"

Olga pulled a cell out of her jacket. "I have good selfie. Happy one." Wonderful picture. Both of them grinning madly at the camera like drinking buddies on the town. Totally wrong for this story.

"Do you have a more serious one?"

Olga frowned but scrolled through more picture files and selected another shot. A selfie again. Taken at the airport, both grim as exhausted refugees.

"Much better. Can you send this to me, and the others?" He

gave her his number. "Once this is published, the police will want to talk to you."

"What do I tell them?"

This was unexpected: Olga willing to take directions.

"What did Yolkov say to get you out of the apartment?"

"That Rudin knew his address and was coming. Because I had no weapon to defend myself, I ran away."

"Any mention of the phone bug?" Zach asked.

"Yes."

"Leave that out. Just say Yolkov was paranoid about you being discovered and persuaded you to leave. He sounded frightened, that made you frightened as well."

"Okay."

Zach rose. "I'll work out a rough draft and show it to you."

"What is rough draft?"

"A first attempt at writing the story."

"There are more attempts?"

"Of course."

"But you are journalist. Why can't you finish story first time? I can do this anytime if I want."

"That's why you're not a journalist."

He reached the door and heard her pushing a drawer shut. "What are you doing?"

"I forget to close," she said as she walked out. "In my country, it's not polite to leave drawer open."

He took her back to the entrance hall. "Why don't you walk around the grounds here. they're spacious and well-tended. Fresh air will do you good."

"Of course," she said, "you want time with your friend. I give you that time."

Zach opened the front door and left it open. The steel gates would be protection enough against intruders. "You are very gracious, and we appreciate this."

"Hah." Olga stalked out, still clutching her bottle.

Keera had given up her paperwork and befriended a bottle of white wine.

"Is Olga driving you to drink?" he asked, sitting opposite her and opening his laptop.

"Even when she's not in the room," Keera said, "her annoying vibes pass through walls. I can't concentrate on anything."

"She's taking a walk outside while I start on her story. I'll join you for a glass or two in a few minutes."

Zach opened the private *Post* web page where he wrote his material directly. Howard could access this, make corrections or add more material of his own. He started with Yolkov's killing, added the information about Olga arriving and escaping death so far, and finished with a tenuous link to Rudin and the data breach at City Hall. It wasn't solid as a case against Rudin, but Edwina now had hard news and was more likely to treat him as a human again.

Best of all, Rudin, like every weasel in the woods, would hate the publicity. At least it would make him more cautious when, or if, he tried to grab him or Keera again. And, of course, Olga.

He uploaded the photographs she'd sent to his phone and captioned them. Added instructions that Olga's face was to be blurred out. Added a note that it was all he had right now, and Edwina should run the Yolkov killing immediately. It'd be a top story on its own.

No other reporter had been on the scene at the exact moment of death, and they would be taking their notes from police reports and bystanders. They could only quote people; he was speaking from direct observation. It was front-page stuff, and for once he wished he hadn't written it. He completed the piece, sent it off to the *Post*, and closed his laptop.

Keera looked up. "What do you think of our Russian queen?" She refilled her glass.

"Combative, sneaky, emotional, all of those things at the same time. Typical for girls of that age. I see you two have hit it off wonderfully."

"Hah," she said and giggled.

The bottle was two-thirds empty already. He slid it out of her reach, and she didn't object.

"Was it fun flying your little toy this morning?" she asked.

"It got to the door fine, then the screen went blank. I heard a gunshot, so I assume they downed it."

"Such exciting times we live in."

He reached across the table and entangled her fingers in his. "The best times of my life, I reckon."

Whatever he expected, all he got was a goofy smile as she stretched for the bottle and refilled her glass.

"Don't you need a clear head for tomorrow?" he asked.

Keera rolled a shoulder, had reached her don't-care-ish stage.

"Didn't you once tell me that your psychic powers won't work with alcohol in your system?"

No reply. The day's events had overwhelmed her. The cozy breakfast they had shared that morning seemed years away. Since then, the killings, the frantic discovery of the bugs, and now the murderous Olga on their patch, and the constant threat of Rudin finding them had overloaded her.

Under the circumstances, the wine was the most convenient

analgesic. She hadn't collapsed into a sobbing, fetal position. It wasn't her style. She had slid into her fatalistic attitude. Whatever happens, happens. Our fate has been determined. Rubbish like that.

Keera lifted her head suddenly. "What are you going to do now?"

Tough question, short answer: he hadn't a clue. "I was hoping," he said, "that you might throw extra light on the situation. You know, ask for guidance from above, that sort of thing."

"Bardo? He doesn't exist above us. Lives in another dimension." She waved an airy hand.

"Wherever he hangs out I figure he'd be interested in helping you, and by extension, us, out of this pickle."

Again, no reply.

Outside, the sky had darkened enough for him to rise and turn on the lights. He peered out the front door but saw no Olga. He found a switch to activate the entrance lights and left the door ajar for her return.

Back at the table, Keera had finished her glass but hadn't refilled it. A good sign. Her hands cupped her chin as if she was contemplating life, or at least a better one than she had endured today.

A sound, a footfall from the entry hall.

Not Olga—a heavier step, a man's step.

Another sound—

The gates clanking open.

CHAPTER 25

The call that changed everything came that afternoon. Rudin listened to his phone; his grin widening with each word.

"Write this address down," he ordered Yuri.

Yes, sir. Certainly, sir. Yuri wrote down the address. Lake Forest. Yuri checked his phone GPS. It wasn't more than twenty minutes away. The street view showed big gates and a high hedge that obscured most of the house. And a glimpse of a curved driveway passing the front door.

"Is this where our lovebirds have flown?" he asked Rudin.

"This property belongs to Nelson Miles, oil executive. My boys say he's listed in the City Hall data as owner, and he pays all taxes on time. Does that sound like a relative of the girl?"

"Her father," Yuri said. " I saw his name in her phone contacts list when we first met."

Rudin turned to Lev. "You and Konstantin, drive over there and make sure it's the right place. Stay until you see either of them, then call me."

"They'll be spotted," Yuri said. "They've both been seen with the van. When they tried to grab the girl and when Yolkov was eliminated."

"Okay. Go rent another van," Rudin said. "Leave the white one near the rental place."

"The police are searching for a white van," Yuri said. "It should stay out of sight."

Rudin rounded on him with some heat. "Fine. You drive the others to the rental place and bring the van back here."

"That will expose the white van to unnecessary risk. What if I drive them in the SUV?"

"*Mater Bozh'ye.*" Rudin pointed to the door which Yuri took to mean he agreed with taking the SUV. He scooped the keys from a side table and led the others out.

"We're taking the SUV," he said to Grigor who was leaning against it, and who glanced at Lev but found no disagreement.

"You always an annoying prick?" Lev asked him as they drove out into the street.

"Somebody has to think through the consequences of every action."

"That would be you, of course."

"If one has the talent, then one must employ it."

"You never think Rudin might be happier to plug you rather than listen to your prissy little arguments anymore?"

"I led him to this million-dollar baby," Yuri said. "That makes a man very forgiving."

"Only for a while, my friend. In my experience, gratitude is a short-lived emotion."

Yuri waited in the street while Lev organized the van rental , then drove off to survey the target house. Rudin hadn't said anything about coming back right away, so he followed the rental.

Lev swept along the street without slowing at the right number, circled the block, and parked fifty yards away, where any car coming and going would be seen. Any pedestrians, of course, were unlikely in this neighborhood.

Yuri cruised a lengthy distance behind him, past the closed gates, but saw no car in the driveway. Bones hadn't rescued his car for no reason, and if he had created a secure base here, he would arrive soon.

Once the couple's presence was verified, both ends of the street could be blocked if they tried to break out. All the houses here were extremely upscale, and escape over other people's gardens was unlikely. Alarms would erupt and guard dogs would bark. Their prey was boxed in.

Yuri returned to the pink house.

"What took you so long?" Rudin barked. "You chose the scenic route? Decided to catch movie?"

"What's the hurry?" Yuri dropped the key on the side table. "We can do nothing until Lev reports back."

"Where were you?"

"I followed him. The place is just like its street view. The hedge maybe a little higher. We can put vehicles at both ends of the street to catch them if we have to."

Rudin lifted a finger at him. "You are not the commander of a tank division; I'll figure out the scenario. For you, I have fresh task. We move from here tonight."

"We have a new safe house?"

"Not yet. You find a hotel suite for a week while we complete the job we came here to do."

"No problem. I book high-quality five-star place. Opulent and classy."

"Get trade rate."

"Of course."

"As soon as this is done, load the car with everybody's bags. When Lev returns, we make our move."

Of course, sir. I'll use my own credit card, sir. Pay me back whenever you want, sir.

The suite booking was secured in no time at all. The most expensive sections of any hotel took the longest to be booked out. The gathering of the group's baggage was more onerous. He moved from bedroom to bedroom, throwing clothes and belongings into suitcases without even considering neatness.

Rudin had also brought a couple of briefcases, one of which he reserved for his laptop, the other for paperwork that didn't interest Yuri. Rudin's luggage he packed with more thought, but not a lot more.

He took them all downstairs and piled them near the front door. The others, well, who knew what hidden vices they had stashed under mattresses, behind curtains—none of which he could be bothered to seek out. He wasn't a maid.

Lev called a short time later.

"They're home," Rudin told Yuri after the call. "Let's go."

Yuri stacked bags in the back of the SUV, and when it was full, he threw the last one on the back seat. Grigor drove them away into the gathering darkness.

He said to Rudin, "You think the female I saw will be there?"

"What you saw," Rudin said, "was only imagination."

"What about that Olga? Will she be there?"

"I don't know, but I hope so; it will make the evening more enjoyable."

Grigor drummed his fingers on the wheel. "I have a bad feeling about her."

Rudin said, "Lucky for us you are only the driver, not our resident counselor. If this Olga is there, we'll take care of her first. She's a nuisance, of no tactical advantage to us."

They pulled in behind the rental van and Lev climbed out to confer with them. "The red Mustang," he said, "arrived, the gates opened, from the inside I think. I saw no remote in his hand. Which means the girl's there also."

Rudin clapped hands together. "Terrific. We have them trapped in their own cage."

"I took a walk up the street a few minutes ago," Lev said. "They've left the front door open and the entrance light on."

"Maybe they're expecting someone," Rudin said.

"It's a trap," Yuri said. "Obvious as hell."

"With the gates closed?" Rudin said. "Not likely."

"It's too obvious to be a trap," Lev said. "The door open, lights on? Bones probably getting stuff out of his car and forgetting to close the door."

"The gates," Yuri said, giving up his argument. "What about the gates? Do we all climb over them?"

"No, Yuri," Lev said. "You won't have to wrinkle your pants. I looked them over as best I could, and I'm sure they're the type that slide open automatically if their power is cut off. People don't like to be trapped inside a burning home, among other considerations. I can buy heavy-duty insulated wire cutters."

"And if they don't open as you say?"

"Then a couple of us will climb them, enter the house, and force our two cuties to open them for the rest of you."

"Excellent," Rudin said. "Let's do that anyway. We have no

time for shopping."

Lev noticed his bag on the back seat. "Who touched my bag?"

"Yuri packed up so we could leave right away," Rudin said.

"I hope I didn't forget your shaving kit," Yuri said.

"Did you collect all my stuff?" Lev getting annoyed.

"I am not your butler. I threw in your clothes that were lying around; maybe I may've mixed them up with Konstantin's. You two can arrange a swap meet later."

Lev drew a deep breath as if to break out with his choice of invectives.

"Enough, boys," Rudin said. "This is what we do. Lev and Konstantin climb over and find internal gate control box; has to be near the door. Open the gates for us to drive in, find those two, and anybody else. There are Christmas presents inside."

Lev tapped the roof of the SUV in agreement, collected Konstantin, and the two of them approached the gates, the SUV following. The gates stood eight feet high, but bore no spikes. Lev linked his hands together in a makeshift stirrup and gave the hefty Konstantin a boost so he could reach the top rail and drop to the ground on the other side.

Konstantin thrust meaty arms through the bars and assisted Lev over in the same way. The two of them moved silently up the driveway, and Lev, gun in hand, stepped inside the house.

Seconds later, the gates jolted into life and rolled open.

CHAPTER 26

Zach was halfway out of his seat when Yolkov's killer walked into the room.

"Sit," he said, pointing a gun. Zach sat.

The killer turned to Keera, "Bad luck for you, no trains run through here."

She regarded him with clouded eyes, and Zach knew she was furious with herself at choosing this evening, of all evenings, to drink alcohol. The wine would have prevented her from sensing the Russians' approach. Her abilities blocked for hours until the alcohol worked its way out of her system.

Another Russian entered the room. Wide as a tank, no visible weapon. He checked the living area for other occupants, then returned to the hall and mounted the stairs.

"Are you staying for long?" Zach asked the killer.

"Ask the boss, he'll be here soon."

"We're having a gathering of like-minded souls?"

"That depends on how you like our plans."

How the hell the Russians had found this place bothered him. He hadn't mentioned the address over his bugged phone. Also damn sure he hadn't been followed after the drone delivery.

A vehicle drew up outside. More footsteps. Rudin entered the room trailed by the goon who'd elbowed his nose at the first meeting, and Yuri.

"How about that?" Zach said. "All the people I admire in the world, gathered in one room. Yuri, I'm surprised you still want to be a friend."

"You have remarkable qualities, Mr. Bones," Yuri replied. "Behaving with respect in the company of your superiors is not one of them."

At their previous meeting, Zach had revealed details of Yuri's private life that had shocked him. Yuri never guessed Keera had collected the information from Yuri's dead relatives. He'd formed the erroneous conclusion, helped along with Zach's suggestions, that a top-secret government agency was always watching Keera. And those who threatened her. Even now, Yuri showed a slight nervousness that more of his precious inner secrets might be spotlighted tonight.

Wide Guy came back from his upstairs search, nodded to Rudin. Elbow Guy said, "I think I saw somebody in the garden when we drove up."

Rudin said, "Take a walk outside with Konstantin, see what you find." The two of them left. Rudin, holding a laptop, moved around the table and sat at the end.

"Dmitri Rudin," Zach said. "How lovely to see you again. I hope you got my note."

Rudin grunted annoyance. Either at hearing his full name or at the sarcasm. Hard to tell with killers and thieves. Zach thought of revealing he knew who was responsible for the data theft but recalled his story on Yolkov's death, and its link to Rudin, would be available online. If not already, then soon. Let Rudin see the story instead. Why take away the thrill of discovery? "To what do we deserve the pleasure of your company?" he asked.

"You know how it is when you start new business," Rudin said. "There are always small difficulties at beginning. Unexpected problems to be ironed out. This is such a moment."

"I rejoice in the opportunity to be of assistance."

"Of course you will assist. Your enjoyment is of no interest."

"What do you want?"

"First, this week's million dollars. After that, we can relax and share feelings."

Zach shot a questioning glance at Keera, but she was locked in a space of her own, and he couldn't penetrate it. He mentally tallied her drinks: four, by his count. That many drinks would take approximately four hours to disappear from his bloodstream. He guessed three had passed since her first drink. That didn't account for her smaller frame Could be another two hours. Nothing sped up the process; time was the only factor.

And where was Olga? Had she taken the opportunity to flee when left unwatched? Or had she bolted when she saw the Russians arrive? Let's hope so.

Rudin slid his laptop around so Zach could see the screen. "That number at the top?" Rudin said. "It's my Bitcoin wallet number. The million, now, please."

Zach drew his laptop closer and booted up. Yuri moved behind him to watch.

"My password is private," Zach said, looking over his shoulder.

"Not anymore," Yuri said. "Call it out as you enter it."

Zach turned to Rudin, who waved an impatient hand at him. Do as you're told, he meant. Zach called out the laptop password and clicked on his Bitcoin wallet. Called out that password as well. Opened the program to display the account details.

"Hey," Yuri said. "He wasn't lying. He's got it, the whole million. Waiting for us."

"Good," Rudin said. "Transfer now, please."

Zach rose and said, "You do it." He came around the table and stood behind Keera. They didn't stop him. Placed a hand on her shoulders and gave her a gentle squeeze.

Yuri sat and tapped Zach's keyboard. "Done," he said.

"Good," Rudin said. "You see how easy it is when the right people are in charge?" He stared at his Bitcoin wallet for a few more seconds, as if he couldn't believe the money had arrived, then closed the laptop carefully and held it to his chest. Like it warmed his very soul.

"You have to move the money immediately," Yuri said. "It's not safe there. Move it to a Bitcoin exchange."

"I watched couple of those outfits close down," Rudin said. "I don't trust them. Later, I'll move it back to dollar account in good bank."

"What if your hard drive fails?"

"Yuri, you are tiresome."

"At least, leave the money in Bitcoins for a while. Their price is rising. Ten percent this week."

On the table, Zach's phone buzzed. A text message.

Rudin reached over, picked up the phone, and read the message. "What does this 'Roy' mean?" he asked Zach. "A short message, even from a friend."

Plenty's secret code. He'd discovered something important

and was waiting for a callback. "It's a colleague," Zach said. "He's seen my story online, I guess, and he wants me to call him."

"What story?"

Time to show and tell. "The one about Yolkov's killing, and how it's linked to the data theft at City Hall, and how interesting it is that you have arrived in Chicago."

"What made you write that stupid story?" Rudin's eyes dark with anger as he dumped the phone on the table.

"The cops asked what I knew of Yolkov and his death. After I told them, there was no reason not to publish."

Rudin nodded to Yuri, who tapped Zach's keyboards again, looked up at Zach, and wordlessly slid the laptop over to Rudin. He read the screen with frowning concentration. Looked up at Zach, "Come here and sit down."

Zach sat next to him. About time Rudin finally grasped a few realities. Now they could discuss issues in a sensible manner and reach an amicable agreement.

Rudin drew back his fist and smashed it into the side of Zach's head. He flew off the chair and hit the floor. Somewhere in the fuzzy background, he heard Keera shriek.

Hands lifted him up, thrust him back into his chair. He focused on the room. Keera staring at him, horrified, held in her chair by Yolkov's killer. Hands patted him on the shoulder, Yuri saying, "What did I say about being respectful? You shouldn't write anything without permission."

Rudin was back to rereading his story. "What you have written about me is all guesswork. You are clever reporter: you say much, but it means nothing. This is only minor irritation, for which your girlfriend will suffer, as well as you." Rudin pushed Zach's laptop away and picked up his own.

The Russian inspected him, calmer, as if he'd figured the next course of action and it pleased him. "Where is Olga Petrova?" he asked.

For a moment, Zach was confused. What did Olga have to do with the money? His throbbing temple didn't make it easy to think straight. As he struggled to respond, the answer came from outside.

Two gunshots.

◆ ◆ ◆

Keera fixed on the doorway, expecting Olga's body to be dragged in and dumped in front of them.

Instead, Olga's body walked right in of its own accord, gripping a small pistol which Keera recognized as her father's. The low caliber weapon he kept in his study desk. The Russian behind her shifted, and she remembered he was also holding a gun, shielded from Olga's view.

She tried to grasp how the next few minutes would pan out. Again, she cursed herself for the wine, for being helpless when she needed to function with clarity. Nothing came to her; worse, the cataclysmic effect of seeing Zach suffer so explosively had destroyed her calming attempts.

Olga had trained her gun on the man behind Keera, aiming high. God knows how good a shot Olga was, how confident of scoring a hit without tearing holes in the wrong body. Hers.

Judging by the number of shots they'd heard, the girl wasn't one for lengthy contemplation. She must have shot the two men outside, one after the other, in seconds. It had been an execution, and Olga was charged by it. Her chest heaved as if a killing frenzy had started. Zach sat numb and distant, like he was still putting his mind and body back together.

"Which is Rudin?" Olga barked.

All three Russians kept their eyes glued on her; no one dared to flick a glance sideways.

"I have disposed of your two useless guards," she said. "I didn't hesitate for one second. I have no fear of death or consequences. I will kill all of you if I have to." She kept her gun on the man behind Keera, but her eyes swept over Rudin and Yuri, both of whom flanked Zach.

"One of you killed my father ten years ago. That person will die now. The rest of you also, if you try to stop this."

Keera didn't dare glance at Rudin and give him away. The man behind her might lift his gun and fire the next time Olga was distracted. This wasn't her psychic ability returning; this was ordinary, chilling logic.

Olga slid a step forward. If she kept approaching, the man had to make a move, and her weapon was already out and a microsecond from firing. If she planned to kill all three intruders, then this one, the one with his hands out of sight, had to be the first. The man behind her moved sideways, keeping Keera's body between Olga and himself.

Keera risked a glance at Zach. Stay quiet, she silently urged. Don't identify Rudin in any way. The room is seconds from Armageddon.

Zach shifted in his seat.

Please, don't distract her.

He lifted his head as if comprehending the scenario for the first time. His eyes were glazed, unfocused, and he was obviously struggling to grasp the situation.

Zach shook his head slowly. Keera knew this action, a mind-clearing thing when he was confused. He'd turn this way and that as if he was rocking thoughts into position.

But his first movement was towards Rudin.

Enough for Olga.

She swiveled to Rudin and fired. The shock of impact toppled him off the chair, still clutching his laptop.

A split second later, a massive explosion in Keera's ear deafened her. Olga stumbled backward, trying to bring her gun hand to bear on the shooter. A second shot blasted her off balance, her legs folded under her and she flopped to the floor, her gun skittering away. Keera didn't have to take Olga's pulse to see she was dead. A bloody red apron spread over her upper chest.

Rudin groaned with pain, but to Keera's amazement, he was struggling to his feet. Yuri helped him upright, then stared at the laptop Rudin still clutched.

"The bullet hit it," Yuri cried in disbelief, pointing at the laptop and its dented lid. When he tried to remove it from Rudin, the Russian wouldn't let go.

"I have to see what your injuries are," Yuri said. "Lev," he said to the gunman. "Help me before he bleeds to death."

Lev left her and eased the laptop out of Rudin's hands. He turned the computer over. "No exit hole. The boss will have a big bruise, that's all. One lucky fucker."

None of them cast a further glance at Olga. Her short angry life extinguished in a split second because of one reason—she'd mistaken her anger for armor.

Keera moved to Zach and placed hands on his shoulders. "Are you all right?" she whispered. He moaned in response, but an encouraging moan. It meant: I feel awful, but I'm not dying.

She wasn't sure how much he understood—he had given away Rudin inadvertently. He'd saved her from being in the middle of a gunfight between Olga and Lev. But he'd caused Olga's death.

Rudin grabbed the laptop back and found his voice. "We go. We take those two, leave all bodies; we don't have time to clean up."

"Leave Grigor and Konstantin?" Lev queried, a dangerous edge to his objection.

"Too much shooting, neighbors will have called cops. We go, go."

"If they are alive," Lev said, "we take them." He left the room before Rudin could object.

"Collect all their phones," Rudin said to Yuri, "and turn them off." Yuri killed the phones and picked up Zach's laptop.

"If you try to run away," Rudin said to Zach, "we will shoot your girlfriend. Understand?"

Zach responded with a barely perceptible nod. To bolster his promise, Rudin reached inside his jacket and pulled out a squarish handgun. "It's impossible to miss with this beauty," he said. "Glock 19, the best." He rubbed off an imaginary speck with a thumb.

Keera caught an unexpected image of him shooting Olga's father, all those years ago. A brief image, but a sign that her psychic strength was returning. "You can see Zach isn't in any condition to cause you trouble," she said. "And I won't leave him."

"Good, good. This is correct attitude."

But I'm not promising that I won't do my best to destroy you.

Lev waited for them by an SUV. "They're dead," he said.

"Murdered by that stupid girl, back of the head. How she got so close, I don't know. At least I avenged them."

That stupid girl? Maybe. But only because Olga was too young to temper her fury with realism. Too angry to wait for the best time and method of revenge. Too late for any of that now.

Yuri said, "Remove all their ID, weapons, and anything in their pockets that the cops will find useful. And then take van back to rental place. It won't be linked to here if you move fast. Get a cab to hotel; I'll message details."

Lev scowled at him and turned to Rudin for confirmation. Rudin shot an angry look at Yuri, but only shrugged and nodded his okay. "Work fast," was all he said.

Lev reached for his bag, pulled out a red t-shirt and strode back into the darkness. Rudin climbed into the back of the SUV, still pressing his laptop to his chest. He gestured for Zach to join him. Yuri pushed him forward, closed the door. He led Keera around to the front passenger door. As she sat inside, Rudin's gun barrel nuzzled her neck.

"Just a reminder of the agreement we have," Rudin said.

She didn't reply.

They reversed down the drive, Lev walking before them until they reached the street. The red t-shirt in his hands, now wrapped around guns and wallets. Yuri turned the car around and took off. No residents on the streets, nobody investigating the gunshots.

There was no profit in being inquisitive.

CHAPTER 27

Yuri drove them to the hotel. Keera waited for any new visions, intimations, anything dammit, to manifest, but nothing showed. Her alcohol level was still too high. Bardo, she asked silently. What do I do?

No reply.

That meant something. Either she possessed everything they needed to escape the situation, or it was the other thing—the one she didn't want to think about. Could Zach be counted on to move fast if necessary, or if he was still dead weight.

"How's your head, Zach?" she asked.

He mumbled something unintelligible. Must have realized this. Tried again. "Still on my shoulders, I think."

"If either of you speak again," Rudin said, "I will bounce gun off both your skulls."

She didn't respond. Zach sounded stronger, sounded like he was aware of the situation. Next thing: find out where they were going. Easy, if they didn't blindfold her or Zach. After that: transmit their whereabouts to the authorities. Somehow. Finally: wait.

A solid plan, the only one, but impossible without help from somewhere, or someone. That would be you, Bardo.

No reply.

"Time for the fancy hats," Yuri said. He reached past Keera to the glove box and pulled out two plastic shopping bags, both black. "Hand one to your useless friend, and put them over heads."

She did as she was told and heard Zach's bag rustling as he covered his head. Breathing was uncomfortable but possible. They would live.

Ten minutes later, the car slowed, turned and descended a few yards. An intercom fuzzed into life, asking if they needed help.

"We are booked for two nights," Yuri said. "Here is the booking code." He read off a string of numbers.

"Thank you," the intercom said, "please proceed."

The car descended further before stopping.

"You two bag-heads will sit here quietly until I return," Yuri said. "There is a gun in back of Ms. Miles's head. The safety is off, Mr. Bones, so this is not a time to be provocative."

Rudin's gun barrel poked her for emphasis.

With Yuri gone, the only sound in the car a tapping on the laptop keyboard as Rudin checked emails, one-handed she guessed, because a gun barrel still rested against her neck. Other cars passed them but none stopped, nor did any passersby make surprised comments on the occupants. Either the windows were heavily tinted, or three people sitting in a car, two of them with plastic shopping bags over their heads, was a familiar sight in these parts.

By the time she heard Yuri's voice again, Rudin had ceased his tapping and was grunting annoyance. Yuri pulled her from the car and removed the bag. Zach climbed out of the other side. Lev steered him around the car, and Yuri removed Zach's bag also.

"Both of you know how this works," Yuri said to them. "We will proceed in a casual manner to our rooms like we're good friends. If either of you run, the girl gets the first bullet. If you signal to anybody, they will also be killed. Please show agreement."

Keera and Zach nodded. She didn't believe they would jeopardize millions with hasty actions, but she wasn't prepared to put the idea to the test. There was nobody in the elevator or the corridor outside the suite entrance.

Nothing in the tired decor suggested a five-star hotel, maybe a sagging four-star. Not a place where the staff paid solicitous attention to the guests; more likely, they ignored any requests for extra service as long as they could. Perfect for Rudin and his merry men.

Nothing gave away the name of the hotel; all she caught was the suite number: 1501. Inside, the red t-shirt lay unwrapped on a coffee table and displayed the pocket contents of the two Russians Olga had killed.

Rudin said to Yuri, "Go back down and bring up our baggage. Lev can help me watch these two."

"Me?" Yuri was hoarse with disbelief.

"You're not a weapons guy; Lev is. I need him here."

Yuri colored but didn't argue further. He left the room.

Lev pushed Zach and Keera into a bedroom. He ran his hands over their bodies and removed Zach's wallet and keys. With her, he took his time, as she expected, but found nothing to interest him that wasn't flesh. She checked an impulse to strike him

223

when he thrust fingers between her breasts and bra cups, but after that, he left her alone without further humiliation. His attitude had been more clinical than sexual.

But her anger subsided only when Zach took her into his arms. "We're still okay," he said. "We can beat this."

His confidence was functioning, his inner strength returning —he was ready to take on three men with four guns, for God's sake. She checked the side of his face: abrasions streaked his cheek where Rudin's knuckles had plowed furrows, but no other bleeding. "Do you have a headache?"

"It's passing. How about you?"

"I keep thinking of Olga. She was a murderous little vixen, but she was totally out of her depth with this lot. So sad."

"I tried to tell her she had no chance," Zach said, "but you saw how she was—fixated on revenge. One thing she did for us though, she reduced the enemy by two men."

He entered the bathroom to inspect his appearance. "If I had to meet these guys every day," he said, staring at the mirror, "I'd invest in a football helmet."

"Better start looking, Zach." Keera leaned against the door. "They'll keep you bclose until you stop producing the money."

Zach rinsed his face delicately and patted it dry. "What about you?" he asked. "You wanna freshen up?"

"Are you suggesting I had too much to drink? Well, I did. I feel so ashamed; I could have sensed they were coming, and we wouldn't be here now."

He held her against him. "If anybody messed up, it was me; I didn't grasp that the data theft meant they could locate your father's property details. We should have moved immediately."

They had both dropped their guard; they had both

underestimated the nature of the Russians. Despite all her advantages, they were now as helpless as anybody.

"Can you think of anything we should do?" she asked.

"I was hoping to stretch out the rest of the money, feed them smaller amounts each week. I thought a few hundred thousand would keep them interested."

"Might buy us time."

Zach released her. "Unfortunately, they have my laptop, and they will scrutinize every keystroke I make. They'll discover the two million in an offshore bank, they'll take it, and then there is no more. And I can't convince them otherwise."

"Do you know where we are?" she asked

"Sure, some dump downtown with a bunch of killers and thieves who think they've just made a million bucks."

What was this? "They haven't?"

"No laptop can withstand a bullet to its workings. It wouldn't boot up. You heard Rudin pounding the keyboard, getting more and more impatient."

"So?"

"If the hard drive is damaged, the money's gone."

"Gone where?"

Zach said, grinning like fuck, "Poof, just gone. The million bucks they thought they had? It no longer exists."

Yuri walked in and dropped the bags, set Bones' laptop on a side table. The last effects of Grigor and Konstantin were piled sat at one end of the table. The two phones belonging to the captives lay separately, and Olga's handbag completed the haul.

He frowned at Rudin and Lev. "Why are these items here?

Have we forgotten basic good sense?"

"Relax," Rudin said from the sofa. "Tomorrow you can take a cruise on the lake and dump it all overboard. We have a bigger problem." He pointed to his laptop. "It won't boot up."

Yuri persisted. "The phones of the living are fine, we might need them. The others are linked to the dead, they have to disappear right away."

"Nobody's coming here tonight, but if you're so worried, why don't you take them and find a new home for them before you sleep."

Yuri took a second to tamp down his anger. Rudin was blatantly baiting him, any minute now he'd belittle him in front of Lev, or even Bones and his girl.

"You want me to drive around in a car that maybe somebody saw at Lake Forest, carrying the guns and ID of the two men being examined by the cops?"

"You're the one who's making a big dance about it."

"Because it's important to do the right thing at the right time."

"Yuri, dump the stuff or shut up."

"It's too late, I'm tired," Yuri said, making his way to the fridge. "Tired people make mistakes. In the morning."

He withdrew vodka and filled a glass. The vodka he'd specifically requested to be on hand when he made the hotel booking. Any thanks for that? No. Both Rudin and Lev had found it and used it well.

"The laptop," Rudin said. "Tell me why it won't start up."

"It's got a bullet in it, that's why. Let me look."

Yuri turned the laptop over and examined the casing. "The bullet entered the base and didn't exit. The screen is intact, so the bullet is lodged in the works."

"Such a genius you are, another Sherlock Holmes."

"I'm only beginning the inspection. I have precision tools, let me open this up." If Rudin kept up his insulting attitude, he'd find a precision tool in his fucking eye.

Yuri withdrew a plastic case from his bag and took it and the laptop to a dining table. Working methodically, he removed several screws and lifted off the back. The bullet stared back at him, squashed flat, pancaked on the hard drive. If there ever was a more shocking sight, he'd never seen it.

A million dollars, the sequence of numbers and letters that determined its existence, was permanently out of reach. In front of him, in plain sight, but untouchable. He could run his fingers over the hard drive for all eternity, but he'd never unlock the money.

He held up the laptop. "Hard drive dead. Money gone."

Rudin's face hardened. "Can't be."

"I told you to park it elsewhere for safety, and now it's all gone."

"Get it back."

"How? The money existed only as information coded on a disk. The disk is destroyed, useless, a piece of twisted metal." He carefully handed the laptop back to Rudin, resisting the temptation to smash it over his head.

Rudin dumped it on the sofa and jumped up. "This cannot be. Find an expert to pull the drive apart and reassemble it in another laptop."

Rudin was insane. Yuri drew breath. "The information is coded in microscopic pieces. Even God, working with all the angels, can't put this back together again. We have lost the money. Forever."

Rudin poured vodka, swallowed it, glared at the laptop. "Some losses you tolerate because they are the cost of doingbusiness. This one's unacceptable."

"I told you to upload the money to a safe place," Yuri said. "Accidents can happen."

"It was no accident. Why wasn't the girl eliminated before she walked in?"

"We'll never know," Lev said. "The answers lie on the front lawn back there."

Rudin rounded on him. "Why didn't you shoot as soon as you saw her?"

"She came in with her gun out, pointing at me, trigger finger shaking. I had no time to get off an accurate shot."

"*Mater Bozh'ye*, you had a fucking shield!"

Yuri cut in. "She was more than a shield, she was our only hold over Bones to produce the money. Lev took the best option."

Rudin swung back to him. "The best option took a miracle to avoid my death."

Yuri wanted to say how the Lord giveth and the Lord taketh away, but Rudin was too steamed up to be philosophical about his loss. Rudin picked up the laptop and stared at the innards, picking with a fingernail at the flat circle that once was a bullet.

Lev said, "If we're right about Bones, then he can find another million to replace it tomorrow, no problem. I know he never handed over everything, he's not such a fool."

Rudin looked up. "Bring them in."

CHAPTER 28

K eera inspected her face in the bathroom mirror, glanced at the toiletries on the shelf, and dismissed them as useless bottles of colored water. She needed real water more than those sketchy skin and hair care promises. Hydration for the body. A cleansing of the spirit.

So stupid to drink wine while they weren't safe. She shouldn't have let Olga irritate her so much. Had she been able to control her emotions, Olga might have lived.

She filled a glass with water and swallowed it. Then poured another. The city had done a fine job of eliminating harmful bacteria in the water supply, but the result was a taste that blended charcoal, mud, and faint traces of organic matter.

But she needed it, no matter how much her palate protested. The alcohol had worked its diuretic skills, draining her organs of vital water. The organs had responded by tapping into the supply of water that surrounded and cushioned her brain, and left her with a headache to remember. She swallowed another glass of the stuff.

Zach still pressed his ear up against the door. Nobody had

the dirty money anymore—what a beautiful outcome. Unless it made the Russians too angry to be reasonable.

"It sounds like they've discovered their hard drive is busted," he said. "Rudin's going nuts."

"They got new plans?"

He moved away from the door. "Not yet, but I bet their attention will be on me real soon."

"So, what are *our* plans?"

"Simple. I'll stick to my explanation of a secret government organization that controls the money, meaning I don't have access to any more. Does that make sense?"

Keera cast back to her brief moment in Rudin and Yuri's presence. The main take away from that event was the bugging, and the Russians already knew they'd been detected.

That left minor facts: that they knew how Zach retrieved his car; that Rudin called his team "boys." Mostly she knew of Petrov's killing and that Yuri was in on it. Not much, but maybe enough to make them more cautious. Especially if Zach convinced them this information was now in the hands of the government.

"Yes," she said. "It makes sense, perfect sense."

"Good," Zach said. "Because it's all we got."

The door opened, and Yuri beckoned.

"Time for conversation," he said, tense, as if *he* were the one in trouble.

She followed Zach to the main room and saw the coffee table piled up with people's belongings. Those of the dead Russians, she supposed, and Olga's bag. Her phone lay alongside Zach's, switched off like his.

Rudin pointed at his damaged laptop on the sofa. "This piece of rubbish is broken. I need money replaced. You will do this now."

"It's not so easy," Zach said, spreading his hands as if that much would be obvious.

"I can make it easy for you," Rudin said. "Easy as you like." He stared at Keera and back at Zach as if making his point to a ten-year-old.

"I'm not being disagreeable," Zach said, "but I don't have access to unlimited bank accounts. The original money was taken from Vronsky and offered back to you as a gesture. There is no more. We don't rob banks to pay off criminals."

"We?" Rudin snorted. "I don't believe that bullshit." He pointed to the side table. "Your machine. Get started."

Keera said, "If you had started your bugging earlier, you would understand how much we know."

Rudin turned to her, his irritation playing large over his face. "Did I ask you question? I do not believe so."

"Your boys," Keera said, deliberately using his term for his hackers, "could have told you Zach was moving his car. Right past those dimwits you hire."

Rudin reddened.

"When we looked into your background, we found enough to keep you off the streets for life. If we advised the police about them."

"Lucky for us you're so friendly," Yuri said.

Keera addressed him. "Yuri, I know you saved me once, and I'm grateful, but your connection to the killing of Mr. Petrov cannot be ignored. Sorry. Being an accessory after the fact is a serious charge. Besides, isn't the law in Arizona waiting to try you on other crimes? And you have the nerve to commit more offenses while on bail?"

Yuri gave nothing away, but she must have made him rethink the value of this moment.

"Your organization," Rudin said, "is stupid. It gathers information but never acts. Why is this so?"

"It's a very peculiar organization. Few people are aware of its existence, even fewer understand its mission."

All the time she'd been speaking she'd become more convinced that somebody else was in the room. She looked about but counted only the three Russians plus Zach and herself. But there was another soul here, maybe in one of the other bedrooms. Definitely. Whoever it was, they were close. Inside the room. She scanned the area, searching for any sign of this person, alive or dead. Nothing.

Rudin said to Zach, "Open your laptop and start repaying me."

The more she scanned, the more her focus narrowed to the coffee table. Bewildered, she ducked her head to peek under it.

"What the hell is she doing?" Rudin said.

Keera straightened and saw Donnie near the door. Oh, she said, it's only you.

Donnie pointed to the pile of phones on the coffee table.

Yes, I know they are there, she said, but I can't pick mine up and call for help. They won't let me, will they?

Donnie drifted closer and touched Zach's phone then tapped his ear. You don't have to pick it up, he said.

For a couple more seconds she remained bewildered, then it came to her—they had an eavesdropper.

Royston Plenty.

She locked eyes on Zach, prayed he'd catch on also, and

recited the room number aloud. "We are still in suite one, five, zero, one. Suite one, five, zero, one. Five people inside. Three armed Russians, and us two."

Zach stared back, baffled as hell, then his face lit up. He got it like she got it. Plenty. It had to be Plenty, the guy who'd removed the Russian bugs from their phones, who must have installed similar software to listen in himself.

Yuri got it as well. "The phones," he screamed at Rudin. "Their people bugged the phones like you did." Rudin blanked at first, then moved faster than anyone would expect. He grabbed both their phones and thrust them under the couch cushions.

"No," Yuri protested. "What if they can still hear us? Drown the phones in the sink."

Rudin took another cushion off the couch and piled it on top of the first one. "Now they can't hear anything"

Yuri looked this way and that, seething. "You believe me now? Now they know exactly where we are. They are coming."

"If they exist, we have an open link to them anytime we want." Rudin fast to adapt to this unexpected setback. "We can bargain."

Keera said, "You can stay and surrender, or you can run. You have no bargaining chips."

"We have you," Rudin said.

"You have us for today, tomorrow, or for several days if we get room service, but after that, all of us will die, because the police will storm the room. You know this."

"You're unusually calm about your death."

"We prefer to die sooner than to wait until you realize there is no more money and kill us anyway. In the meantime, we would find your company loathsome."

She scanned the room for Donnie, maybe he could suggest a plan, but he had gone. The guy had done something right for a change and left without waiting for thanks.

Yuri checked the corridor as if expecting a SWAT team outside it. "This isn't a time to plan a new strategy. Let's get out of here."

Lev was already holding his bag in his left hand. The other one gripped his final, steely choice of defense. "Whatever we do," he said, "we do it fast. They would have known of this location for only a few minutes. We have time to clear out."

Rudin said, "They only got a suite number, not a street address. She didn't reveal it. We stay here for now. It'll take hours to knock on every door."

"What if they have a GPS operating?"

"They won't. It's not yet available on this software, it's been promised for the next upgrade."

"They don't need it with this software." Yuri was almost screaming. "They could have installed a Find My iPhone app. Or an Android copy. They could have been following their movements for days. Which explains a lot. The only thing their people didn't know was the floor we were on. They do now." He paused to grab a fresh breath. "We have to go."

Rudin said, "We don't."

"You think so?" Yuri reached into the coffee table pile and withdrew an automatic. Racked the slide to chamber a bullet. Pointed it at Rudin. "Are you coming, or staying?"

Rudin didn't respond. Not verbally anyway, he didn't have to. His whole body vibrated in fury. Yuri had only difficult choices in front of him. Either he pulled the trigger now, or Rudin would tear his head off later. Either way, Yuri had just published his death notice.

Behind him, Lev shifted and Yuri swung around. He said to Lev, keeping his aim at Rudin's chest, "You raise your gun, I shoot him."

"This is not helpful," Lev said. "Personal feelings should be put aside. Time to move quickly."

"This bungler brought us here. Never listens."

"I'm listening now," Rudin said. "I'm listening to a crazy man terminating our relationship."

"I'm making sure you don't stop me leaving," Yuri said. "What about you, Lev?"

"We all have to leave," he said.

Yuri sidled to the sofa, picked up Rudin's laptop with his free hand and dropped it on his bag. His gun never wavered from its target.

"You want the laptop you said was useless?" Rudin asked. "You think I'm a fool."

"Who knows what advances technology will bring? Maybe the money can be recovered."

"So you're stealing my money."

"It's called safekeeping."

Lev hadn't moved, made no attempt now to stop Yuri as he picked up Zach's laptop from the side table and rested it on top of the broken one.

"What do you want that for?" Rudin asked.

"There's gold in here, I'm sure of it." Yuri turned to Lev, "Put your gun away. I have to pack these, and I want to be sure of your intentions."

Lev flicked a glance at Rudin, but the boss didn't take his eyes off Yuri. Lev complied, slipping the gun into his waistband.

Yuri, working with one hand, his other gripping his gun, unzipped his bag, worked the two laptops in, zipped up again.

"Time to go," he said to Rudin. "You will stay, as you prefer, but we can't be friends anymore. Lev, you can make your mind up, but I'm leaving."

"I'm coming with you," Lev said. He met Rudin's eye and shrugged the confirmation that Rudin's time as leader was over.

Yuri edged backward, dropped his bag to free a hand, and opened the door. Peeked out. Rudin sensing this was his last chance, flew at Yuri.

Fast as he was, strong as he was, and even though he grabbed Yuri in a bear hug, he couldn't remove Yuri's finger from the trigger. Maybe he'd assumed Yuri wouldn't shoot, that he was only a complaining fusspot.

Wrong. Yuri was soft as iron.

The first shot punched Rudin in the stomach, shredding vital organs. The second ripped his heart apart, and he slid to the floor.

Yuri stood over him, ready to complete the execution. He pressed two fingers against Rudin's neck, then straightened, satisfied.

"You," he said to Zach. "I come back for you another day. Be cooperative next time."

He strode out the door.

Lev followed without a backward glance.

CHAPTER 29

They stood in silence for a long, shocked minute before Keera nudged Zach. "Your phone. Tell the listener what's happened before the police come in shooting."

She was right. If the cops were close, they wouldn't wait any longer, not after hearing gunshots. They'd send in their trigger-happy cowboys. Who knew if they could tell the difference between kidnappers and victims at first glance?

He tossed the cushions aside and held his phone to his ear. Nothing. "It's dead," he said.

"It's not," Keera said, stepping carefully around Rudin's body and resting a hand on Zach's shoulder. "Just tell him what's happened."

"It's Zach," he said, "You know my voice. Two Russians bolted after killing the boss. We're fine, waiting for the cops in the suite. Tell them not to shoot."

Keera patted his back as if he'd just completed a tough assignment. The tough part was remembering how to act normally again. She drew him away from Rudin's body, sat him at the dining table, sat next to him, held both his hands. "Now we wait," she said.

"You think there'll be more killing?"

"I'm sure of it." His thoughts drifted back to the house. When Olga had fired at Rudin. "Why'd Olga try to shoot Rudin, when she had that other guy's gun on her?"

Keera inspected the floor before answering. "She knew she could die any second. Once she identified Rudin, she tried to kill him."

"How did she identify him?"

More floor inspection. "She didn't," she said. "You sort of did."

"Me?"

"Unwittingly. When you were still loopy from that punch in the head."

"I don't recall pointing him out."

"When she asked which one was Rudin, you shook your head slowly, like you do when you want to clear your thoughts. I'm guessing that Olga assumed your head turning in Rudin's direction was a signal."

Zach stared at her, stricken.

Keera squeezed his hands. "You had no idea what you were doing. Once she walked into the room, she was going to be carried out. You and I both know that."

"But still. Jesus." He rubbed his forehead.

"You were an unintentional part of a process that was always going to play out like it did." Keera rose and opened the suite door fully. "Let's not have the police bursting in all tense and nervy.

"You saying she had no chance?"

"Once she decided to kill for revenge, she gave up life. Just like

Yuri did

Zach considered this. "I have to think on this, but not now." He nodded at the open door. "You think they'll get away?"

She didn't answer. She didn't have to.

From somewhere far below them and out on the street: two shots. Then the faint burst of automatic gunfire. Men shouting, then several more bursts.

"Sounds like the police don't want them alive," Keera said.

Sounds like she doesn't care.

When the street below fell quiet again, Zach turned on his phone, waited for the boot-up sequence to complete all tasks, dialed Plenty's number.

"Did we guess right about you?" he asked a void.

Plenty said, "Is everybody okay? It's been damned nerve-wracking listening in."

"We're fine. Nothing rest and alcohol won't cure. When did you bug me?"

"When you didn't respond to my urgent signal. Good call, eh?"

"How much did you hear?"

"An angry girl talking with an accent, then three shots. I immediately notified the authorities. I tracked you all moving to a new location, a hotel, gave them the GPS coordinates, but we didn't know the room number until another female began calling it out. The Russians discovered the bug, obviously, and muffled the phone. Two more shots, faint but gunshots, and I passed that information on also. It was a stressful time after that, I can tell you. I had no idea what was happening."

"We thank you."

"Make sure you tell the cops you authorized my bug on your

phone, will you? They get finicky about that sort of thing."

"Sure."

"And Zach? I don't think you told me the whole truth about these people."

Plenty sounded a little peevish about this, which was cheering.

"That makes two of us with secrets. I'm sure you'll understand."

"The thing is, I usually set my fee according to the size of the problem. I assumed I was hired to perform a location job, to facilitate a news story. It turns out, the main issue here was a million dollars in the wrong hands."

"Life is full of surprises, don't you think?"

"Some of them can be easily adjusted with agreeable bookkeeping."

The guy was angling for more of the cake, and the bodies were still warm, for God's sake. "If you heard the conversations," Zach said, "you'd know the million has disappeared into the ether. There is nothing left of it."

"Not my doing."

"You should also take into account I was trying to give the money away, not get hold of it."

"Not happy, Zach."

New sounds from the corridor: boots thudding on carpet.

"The SWATs are here, Roy. Send me your invoice and let's meet for one of those convivial drinks soon. And make sure any records of what you heard are deleted." Zach killed the phone before Plenty renewed his claim to a non-existent million. Some guys.

More boots shuffled up to the door.

"Come on in fellas," he called. "The party's over. Mind the body by the door."

A mini drone buzzed in from the corridor, made a pass around the room, its camera scanning. Zach waved. The drone zipped out and a cop filled the doorway, side on, full armor, gun extended.

"This room's clear," Zach said. "And so is that one." He pointed to the bedroom he and Keera had occupied. "I have no idea what or who is in the other one, or the bathroom. But we came here with three Russians. One is now on the floor, and the other two ran off."

The cop strode past them and flanked the closed bedroom door Zach had indicated. More cops joined him, crowding in, fanning out, checking all the other rooms. A big boot smashed the closed door open; two cops jumped inside, emerged seconds later exhaling disappointment.

A new cop said to Zach, "I need to check you for weapons, sir. Please hold your arms away from your body."

"You think they'd let me keep any gun?"

"No, but they might wire you up with explosives."

The searcher cleared Zach and motioned for another cop to perform the same task on Keera. This one was female, thank God, and she was as brisk as her colleague.

Medics entered and knelt next to Rudin's body.

"So," Zach asked the searcher cop, "what happened to those other guys? You get them?"

"Ask the detective when he gets here. I have no authority to discuss events."

The detective was Detective Sergeant Declan Gilley, a short man, the shortest you could be and still get into the Chicago

Police Department. However, every other cop in the room altered their posture when he walked in. Gilley carried an attitude that made people pay attention.

He introduced himself, asked for their names, and said, "I take it neither of you was harmed?"

"Not here," Zach answered. "Some rough stuff in Lake Forest when these guys burst in."

"There's been a report of an incident in there," Gilley said. "You involved with that?"

"If it's the same one, yes. That's where the whole abduction thing started."

"Three bodies found there, two bodies here and an earlier, apparently related, death from a shooting in a street." Gilley studied his face. "Not a stat that pleases me."

"Two bodies here? You mean two downstairs and one in this room? I count three."

"I know how to count, Mr. Bones. One man burst out a delivery entrance holding a gun and didn't obey lawful commands to drop it. He was shot dead. We understand there were two Russians who were fleeing, but we haven't found the other one yet. He is presumed to be in the building."

Keera asked, "What color hair did the dead man have?"

"He was a blond," Gilley said.

Yuri.

Lev still on the run.

"What does the other one look like?" Gilley asked.

Zach said, "His name is Lev. Tall, dark hair. jeans, black leather jacket. He told me he used to be a marksman in the army. Be careful, he's already killed two people. He doesn't miss."

Gilley moved to a SWAT guy and murmured something to

him. The guy jerked a radio out of his belt and walked out of the room, relaying instructions to his team. He returned to Zach. "Tell me, is this the start of something or the end of it?"

"You tell me, Detective, you tell me."

"Out of curiosity," Gilley asked, "what was the beef? You're a reporter, right?"

Here it was: the first tricky hurdle. Get the opening statement wrong and the cops would notice, and worry you to death about it. If Rudin's laptop was busted, it helped. But the other laptop held incriminating evidence of illegal money activities. If the cops suspected he was holding information back, they'd get an order to allow them access to his files. After that, well, let's not think about it.

"That guy over there," Zach said, pointing at Rudin with his chin, "was very peeved about a story I wrote. Wanted satisfaction."

"And one of his guys disagreed, and shot him?"

Gilley quick to see the flaws not painted over.

"They argued constantly," Zach said. "Often in a mix of Russian and English, not always easy to understand. I think the guy who shot him and ran, was unhappy about a whole bunch of issues. The other guy, Lev, had no reason to stay behind."

Gilley regarded him with that cynical air all cops must be born with. Kept a long silence going until Zach couldn't help but break it.

"They stole my laptop," he said. "Did you recover it?"

Gilley raised eyebrows. "Six bodies, soon to be seven, I assume, and you want me to worry about your personal computer?"

"Detective, I'm in the middle of the best story of my life. It started yesterday with a fatal sidewalk shooting by one of these men, and it's ended here. I have to file it ASAP. Do you have my laptop?"

Two guys in plain clothes, carrying cases, walked in, nodded to Gilley, and one of them spoke to the medics. Gilley went over to speak to the new guys. Zach took that brief moment to put an arm around Keera as if he was comforting her.

"Don't mention the million," he murmured. "Or we won't be home for supper, for years." He didn't expand on his fears, but she knew what they faced if the whole truth came out.

Gilley saw him with Keera and waved him away from her. "Can you sit over there, Miz," he said to her "I'll talk to you in a minute."

He turned to Zach. "Start from the start. Tell it all."

Zach figured it would be easy to steer the early questions into space. It'd be the double-checking, the cross-checking, that might cause trouble later. "The Russians had killed a guy this morning who had tipped me off about their data theft activities. I don't know how they found this out, but because of the data theft, the Russians were able to locate me at Lake Forest, and dropped by to exact punishment."

"That's where you live?" Gilley asked.

"My girlfriend's parents' house."

"They knew you would be there at the exact time they came along? Gee, they were good."

"They had also bugged my phone. Rudin boasted of it." Another unverifiable piece of nonsense. Zach pointed to his head. "They knocked me about. I may have problems sorting all this information in the right order."

"No problem. You tell me what you know, and I'll do the

sorting."

Zach started with a tipoff about Russians targeting places in Chicago.

"Who told you this?" Gilley interjected.

"Can't tell you." Because I just made it up.

Zach went on to relate the tragic story of Yolkov's death and Olga's rescue, the Russians busting in, Olga's angry slaughter of two Russians before she was killed, and the flight to the hotel.

"Why would they bring you here?" Gilley asked. "Why not kill you two at Lake Forest?"

"I'm not sure. Like I said, they jabbered in Russian quite a lot. They were very keen to find out who tipped me off. I assumed they were going to apply extra pressure once we left the crime scene. Glad it didn't happen."

Gilley wasn't eager to probe more deeply at this stage. He was taking Zach's answers at face value, and there was little chance of his tale being contradicted. All the possible contradictions were now lifeless. He wanted to ask about the laptop again but didn't want Gilley's curiosity aroused. Get one of their tech guys poking around and they'd discover more worms to investigate.

Gilley left him and spoke to Keera for several minutes. She could claim with perfect sincerity that she "was affected by alcohol when the invasion occurred, and couldn't recall anything much, Detective."

When a photographer arrived to document the crime scene, Gilley let them go. "You may find our people still at Lake Forest," he said. "I'll be over tomorrow. We'll talk more."

"Looking forward to it," Zach said, putting his arm around Keera's shoulders and walking her out of the suite.

CHAPTER 30

As the cab drove them away from the hotel, from the death room, past the milling cops around the carpark entrance, past the small crowd gathered to watch them, Keera rested against Zach's shoulder and asked Bardo, is it over yet?

Indeed, and jolly well done. Only the tidying-up left.

She should have relaxed at hearing this but for Bardo's habit of underplaying future events; especially ones she would find harrowing.

What kind of tidying up? she asked warily.

General housekeeping. Fingerprint experts always leave a mess. Nobody puts chairs back either. Bloodstains, of course, and a certain person's chakras need adjusting.

Zach gone quiet since they left the murder suite, and she put that down to sheer relief at leaving that killing room. But Bardo was saying there was a hemorrhaging of his spirit force. She'd better sort that out before he found a more comfortable, but short-lived, remedy in the bottle. He's gloomy about his laptop, she told Bardo. Need he worry?

246

Unpredictabilities have to play out.

God. When will he know his future for sure?

Why should he have an advantage few others in your world have?

Zach deserves it; he works for good.

He doesn't want it, doesn't need it. He's got you.

The reminder filled her with unexpected warmth. And Bardo was right. Zach was grounded in the physical; if he developed his psychic side, he might come adrift from his familiar world. Not a good idea in his profession. It was hard enough for *her* to manage two worlds.

The money. The money needed to find a new home, fast. Its presence had brought death, it had attracted the worst of the worst, and it had to go. Twenty charities to receive a hundred thousand each from an anonymous donor. In Bitcoin. Their source untraceable. She'd insist on it when Zach recovered tomorrow.

She expected no arguments. He'd know by now he was no match for those who'd killed without hesitation. Nobody in a normal world could anyone hope to outwit those who played by different rules. Especially if they made up new ones every day. Damn that money. It had nearly undone them both.

A lone police officer stood outside the gate at Lake Forest when they alighted. His probing flashlight inspected them.

"No visitors today," he said, holding the light on their faces.

"We live here," Keera said, throwing the angriest glare she owned. "Detective Gilley is coming to meet us. Inside."

She stalked past him, Zach following.

"Don't touch the crime scene," the cop yelled after them.

The main area was taped off. Small flags dotted the floor. Three marked the place where spent shells had lain, she guessed, by their random placing. More flags circled a massive bloodstain, Olga's final earthly traces.

Bardo was right: the chairs were strewn about, gray powder littered the tabletop. Her laptop lay in the same place, untouched. The almost empty wine bottle also; an unwelcome reminder of her earlier helplessness.

Movement at the corner of her eye. A slim blonde figure stalked past them, halted in the middle of the bloodstains. And vanished.

Olga.

No. Please no.

Keera waited, but Olga didn't reappear. But she'd be back. She might not even be aware she was dead. Her extreme level of anger at the instant of her death was enough to anchor her to her death moment forever. To endlessly relive her shooting and her exit from her physical world until Keera did something about it.

Well, she could wait until morning. Banishment required a clear head and a purified spirit. Right now, Keera possessed an acute shortage of both.

Footsteps sounded behind them, and a man said, "I heard you were back here. I thought I'd drop by and eyeball the scene."

Zach said, without enthusiasm, "Hello, Detective Kolacz. May I introduce Keera Miles?"

"Pleased to meet you," Kolacz said.

"Not so pleased to meet you," Keera responded tartly. "I thought the questions were done with."

"More questions keep arising."

"Are you working this case also?" Zach asked.

"I'm taking over the whole of the investigation. This

morning's killing and these, are related, aren't they?"

"As I explained to Gilley, yes."

Kolacz peered into the crime-soaked area. "You're a harbinger of death, Bones. Six dead this day alone, and if the last guy running doesn't have sense, it'll be seven. I'm getting nervous in your company."

"This isn't your residence is it?" he asked Zach.

"It belongs to my parents," Keera said. "Zach was visiting when the Russians came."

"Amazing coincidence, don't you think?"

"I appreciate you need to investigate, but we're both exhausted. We've witnessed several killings at close range, been interviewed earlier, answered the same questions then." Her voice rose as she continued. "We are not the killers, we are only witnesses, and we almost became victims."

In her mind, a rat scampered in a maze, this way and that, trying to find the exit and the reward that came after.

Zach said, "They took my laptop when they ran. I need it. Where is it now?"

"Laptop?" Kolacz smiled like he was delivering good news. "The SWAT guys recovered two of them. Which one was yours? The one with three bullet holes, or the one with seven?"

The maze grew clearer; no exit existed. Kolacz was wasting his time.

"Detective," Keera said, "shall we reconvene here in the morning?"

Kolacz asked Zach, "I haven't been able to stop thinking about your phone, swaddled up like an abandoned marsupial in your trunk. I think I should take a close look at it."

"Can't let you," Zach said. "Journalist privilege, and all

that. Police access to my contacts lists would expose many to unwelcome attention."

"I could make you."

"Sure, bring me a warrant from the Supreme Court where it says that you, and you alone, can defy the Constitution."

"What if I take you to the station, and ask questions for the rest of the night, and long into the next day."

"You're kidding," Keera said.

Kolacz smiled at her. "I have a lot of discretion in this matter."

Keera drew herself up. "This is what you have: two witnesses that observed close up the murder of three people—the *only* witnesses you have. Another two victims died only yards away, and we heard the confirmation of this. We'll also supply the motives for all killings. We're all you need to wrap this case up and go on vacation. Ask yourself this: do you want our help or not?"

Kolacz eyed her with contemplation. Must have been deciding whether to push the full authority of his office to get what he wanted, or whether he preferred willing witnesses on the stand later on.

"You're tired," he said, "and not making sense. Why don't I come back in the morning? Until then, don't cross those tapes."

He walked out slowly, like leaving was his idea all along.

Keera closed the door behind him and took Zach upstairs.

"Shall I grab wine from the fridge?" Zach asked.

"You heard the man, don't cross the tapes."

"They'll never find out."

"You know something? After today, I've had all the wine I want for a long time."

"We're free of them. It's over, isn't it? Tell me it's over."

"It's over, Zach. All over."

"Then we need closure. Wine, beer, champagne. God invented them just for this moment." He was trying to spark into life, but there was no fuel left in him.

She wrapped her arms around him and kissed him softly. "We don't need them; we have each other. We calm each other, we invigorate each other, and we renew each other."

He had no answer for that, no strength to maintain any argument. He was done. She led him into her bedroom and lay him on the bed. Removed his shoes, tossed them in the corner.

"First," she said, "I'll cleanse your spirit. Then I'll attend to your body. What do you think of that?"

But he was already asleep.

She wanted to hold him close, bind him to her for safety, and for other things. But he needed sleep. To start the recovery, to bring him back to who he once was, to make him whole again.

She thought of all the time it would take. And the toll of the past few days had taken on him. And her. She thought of Bardo, and his airy assertion it was all over bar the tidying. The tidying of things left undone. At first, she had assumed he was only referring to immediate matters, but a new image kept growing until she couldn't ignore it.

Lev.

The one who got away.

She saw him running, jumping, never standing still. She saw something else, too.

He would never forget the money.

THE END

ACKNOWLEDGEMENT

As always in the process of fiction creation, there are others who labor to make the author appear better than he thought he was.

My thanks go to the members of the Internet Writers Workshop for their perceptive comments and suggestions. In particular, I'd like to acknowledge Robin Cain, Francene Stanley, and Tim Sharp who stayed with this work from the first chapter to the final one.

Some sections of this novel previously appeared in a short story entitled Even When He's Dead.

Parker Rimes

BOOKS BY THIS AUTHOR

The Backward Time Traveler

Keera Miles, a psychic, has a mission. To travel back 200 years and rescue a sacred stone from a Sioux tribe before it's lost forever.

She teams up with an annoying, cynical reporter Zach Bones. Not that he believes her story, but, because he's hiding from a loan shark, because he needs a good story, and because Keera is so gorgeous, he agrees to help her.

The ingenious, twisty plot follows the pair as they adapt to Indian bodies; become trapped in a ferocious Crow raid; and their plan to snatch the stone from the wily and ruthless Red Leaf grows increasingly desperate.

When they escape back to the present, they find they have fled one nightmare for a worse one.

Amazon Customer reactions:

"Fast-paced. Plenty of unexpected humor pops up. Loved reading it."

"Quite a page-turner, with plenty of action, entertaining plot twists, and flashes of unexpected humour."

"Plenty of thrills here, but I didn't expect the humor. Made me laugh out loud."

"What an imaginative and thrilling journey."

The Upside Of Death (Paranormal Crime Book 1)

What happens when a psychic gets kidnapped? When psychic

abilities are the only defense against physical violence. What if you know more about your kidnappers than they know about each other? What if access to the afterlife is all you have to keep you alive?

The Art Of Dash (Paranormal Crime Book 2)

When Chicago journalist Zach Bones incriminates a major drug dealer Jason Virgil, he discovers he's been set up. Virgil is killed in jail on the orders of his rival Frankie Ritchie, and Zach's now a suspect.
Worse, the dead and wrathful Virgil begins to extract revenge on everybody involved. Zach's psychic girlfriend Keera can save him, she thinks.
But after Virgil murders his killer by psychic attack, she realizes that no human can stop him.

Never Show Them Money (Paranormal Crime Book 3)

When too much money is not nearly enough. Zach Bones, a reporter on the Chicago Post, has liberated three million dollars from a Russian kidnappers' bank account. Now he's offering the money to a rival syndicate in grateful payment for them eliminating his psychic girlfriend's kidnappers.
Trouble is, these Russians believe that if he took money out of one bank account, he could do it again. For them. And forever.
Even worse, the hot-headed Olga arrives in town determined to avenge her father's past death at the hands of these Russians.
While Zach searches for a solution, his girlfriend Keera enlists

the aid of her spirit guide Bardo, whose enigmatic advice is hardly better than no advice at all.

The Darker You Get (Paranormal Crime Book 4)

Reporter Zach Bones still has Russian mob money. He'd like to keep it; his psychic girlfriend Keera says give it away—it's dirty.
A hitman Lev wants it also and uses a sniper rifle to make his point. The cops can't understand why a hitman would target an ordinary reporter, and grow suspicious of Zach's lack of explanation.
He can't find a solution that leaves him with a life worth living. And Keera's abilities can only do so much to protect both of them. Especially when Lev is steadily losing his grip on reality.

Eye Of The Beholder: A Novella

Zia checks out a dating website. It lets her view her prospective soulmate's world through his eyes. She sees blue skies. Leafy trees. A car interior. And a pair of feet—chained together. Puzzled and concerned, Zia searches for the truth in the glossy world of people-matching, and uncovers disturbing surgical

procedures.
Worse, her bestie is involved...

Amazon Customer reactions:
"I really enjoyed this book! The concept of being able to see what someone else is seeing would be amazing and freaky all at the same time! I'm glad that I read this book on this beautiful snowy day."
"My previous experience with novellas was that character depth and all the important details were glossed over, but this story was perfectly written."

Catch Your Death: A Novella

There's weird, and there's seriously weird. One of them can really wreck a girl's evening. And every evening after that.
Reporter Ruby Moskewitz is interviewing a famous Professor of Biology when he vanishes during a meal break. Just like that. Has this anything to do with his new drug that accelerates brain?
When she contacts his university she's told the professor has a contagious condition and had to be isolated urgently. This is a lie, she knows it, and she investigates.
Her one advantage? She's in sole possession of the drug that gifts normal people with abnormal powers.

ABOUT THE AUTHOR

Parker Rimes

Parker Rimes has spent his life in Europe, Australia, the UK and the US. When not writing, he likes to read four or five books a week. Some of them he completes.
In the course of his journalist life, he interviewed over a thousand people who claimed paranormal experiences occurred in their homes. Many of these stories seemed truthful.

Diligent research for his novels led him to enroll in a school for mediums, where he failed nearly every psychic test. But he can now predict where to find a good parking space slightly better than the average person.

His favorite pastime is discovering new verbs, and wishing he'd thought of them first.

He likes animals but prefers that most of them stay in their own home. His favorite wines are those sold close to wherever he lives.

His latest musings can be found at www.parkerrimes.com

www.ingramcontent.com/pod-product-compliance
Lightning Source LLC
Chambersburg PA
CBHW011436170626
46808CB00009B/3068